The Woods of Adventure

Jack lost no time in examining the fireplace. It was quite large enough for a man to stand upright in, and it accommodated the four children with ease.

"What exactly are we looking for?" asked Dinah.

"A lever or a handle of some sort," Jack replied. "Or a stone that moves when it's pushed."

"Well, there's no lever," said Philip, who'd examined every square inch. "So let's try pushing all the stones."

As he spoke, Lucy-Ann pushed one of the decorative studs. "This one moves! Look!" she gasped.

They all stared in astonishment as the entire fireplace and grate slid silently backwards to reveal a dark passage.

*There are eight screenplay novelisations
starring Philip, Dinah, Jack and Lucy-Ann from the
Channel Five Enid Blyton™ Adventure Series:*

*All published by
HarperCollinsPublishers Ltd*

Enid Blyton's™

The Woods of Adventure

Screenplay novelisation by
Helen Wire

Collins

An imprint of HarperCollinsPublishers

Original screenplay by
Rio Fanning.

This screenplay novelisation first published
in Great Britain by Collins 1997
1 3 5 7 9 10 8 6 4 2

Collins is an imprint of HarperCollins*Publishers* Ltd,
77-85 Fulham Palace Road, Hammersmith, London W6 8JB.

Copyright © Enid Blyton Ltd 1997

ISBN 0 00 675311 6

The author asserts the moral right to be
identified as the author of this work.

Printed and bound in Great Britain by
Caledonian International Book Manufacturing Ltd,
Glasgow, G64

CHAPTER ONE

"Urgh!"

A fierce pain shot through the hiker's head and shoulders. He reeled back from the castle door, his face white with shock. Looming over him was a terrifying creature shrouded from head to foot in the dark woollen habit of a monk. Mad eyes burned and glittered from the shadowy depths of its all-enveloping hood.

The hiker staggered backwards, his breath coming in rapid, heavy bursts. The awful creature lunged towards him, its arms outstretched.

"NO!" A woman's agonised scream rent the air. "No, Gary! No!"

The ghastly creature hesitated.

The hiker ducked beneath the wavering hands and ran as fast as he could. He could hear the pounding footsteps of his attacker close behind him. As he stumbled on, the woods rang with the woman's shrieking, and another voice – a man's. Both were issuing the same useless command, "Stop Gary! STOP!"

The hiker was fit and, despite the weight

on his back and the wild thumping of his heart, he was fast. He whipped through the undergrowth, leaping over fallen trees and tangled roots. Low hanging branches slapped unheeded against his face. He had to make it back to the gap in the wall.

But he made a fatal mistake – he looked over his shoulder.

The creature was the first to reach his body. It was sprawled awkwardly, face down on the ground, and was deathly still. His head lay pressed hard against a large jagged rock.

"No!" the old woman sobbed when she reached them. "Oh, Gary, no!"

CHAPTER TWO

"Mind your fingers!" squawked Kiki. The white parrot fanned up the yellow crest on her head in a roguish plume, and gave Jack a wink with one of her beady black eyes.

"Yeouch!" Jack yelped and rapidly shook his hand to ease the pain. He glared at Kiki. "You did that on purpose, you dratted bird," he chided, nursing the thumb he'd hit with the mallet as he hammered in the last of the tent pegs.

Turning his back on Kiki's wild cackles, Jack gave the tent peg one final thwack. Then he announced, "Well, that should do it. Not even a hurricane could shift this now."

Dinah Mannering and Jack's sister Lucy-Ann, who were inside the tent rolling out ground sheets and sleeping bags, snorted with amusement when they heard Jack's proud boast. Dinah stuck her head out of the entrance flap and raised her eyebrows in mock seriousness. "Expecting a hurricane then, are we, Jack?"

Jack glared at her, but before he could think of a smart retort, his sister's disembodied voice declared from inside the tent, "Oh goodness! I hope not!"

"What I'd really like to do," he said dreamily, his eyes lingering on the wooden garden furniture, "is build a fire. Just think, we could barbecue fish, fry sausages, bake potatoes—"

"For heaven's sake, Jack!" interrupted Dinah with a hint of exasperation in her voice. "We can't possibly make a fire on the lawn. It would kill the grass."

Jack glared at her again. What a spoilsport she was! Why did she always have to point out even the most minor of flaws in his brilliant ideas?

"Well," he said grumpily, "what's the point of a camp without a fire?"

Dinah crawled out of the tent and stood in front of him with her arms crossed. She was almost the same age as Jack, but whereas Jack was small and wiry, Dinah was chunky and tough.

"Listen, you twit," she said, "we're hardly in the wilds of outer Mongolia. We're on the Craggy Tops lawn, and two lickety-split steps away from a kitchen, a fridge . . . and a cooker!" she added with pointed emphasis.

"But it's not the same," moaned Jack. "Honestly, Dinah, just think what we could do with a good fire. We could toast marshmallows. Or roast a chicken on a spit, or—"

At that moment, they all heard the distant screech of an owl. Jack, who was completely batty about birds, cocked his head in the general direction of the call.

"I think," he said excitedly, "that was a long-eared owl."

Behind him, Dinah suddenly screamed.

Jack looked back at her in astonishment. "It's only an owl," he said. "It won't hurt you."

"Get it off. Get it off. Get it off," she whimpered, almost unable to breathe, let alone speak.

"But it's miles away, silly— Oh!"

Lucy-Ann, who wasn't the least bothered by creepy crawlies, had just then rescued Dinah from the spider that Philip, Dinah's brother, had quietly plopped on to the back of her hand.

"You're rotten, Philip!" Dinah gasped, "You know how I hate spiders. One of these days I'll . . . I'll . . ."

"I know, I know. You'll be thanking me!

11

It's called aversion therapy, you know!" He grinned. "Anyway," he continued, "what's so awful about spiders?" He was truly curious to know. He simply couldn't imagine why anyone would, or could, dislike a single living creature.

"Oh, I don't know," she said wearily, "I just can't bear the horrid things."

"But they're completely harmless," Philip continued.

"I know that. But it didn't feel harmless to me," she snapped.

"Oh, cut it out, you two!" interjected Jack. "It'll ruin the whole evening if we keep arguing like this."

"It was only a joke," protested Philip.

"Well, it wasn't funny, and I'm not laughing," said Dinah.

Lucy-Ann tried to distract them. "Do you think Kiki might like this little morsel?" She held out the offending spider.

"Don't you dare!" said Philip. He took it gently from her hand, and was releasing it into the safety of the nearby rockery, when he heard his mother's Land Rover scrunching up the gravel drive. All the children rushed to greet Alison as she drew up in front of the house.

"Hello, you lot. Everything all right?" she said, as she stepped down from the big four-wheel-drive. The children pointed to the lawn. "Hey! Pretty nifty-looking tent, kids!" she said, her voice full of admiration. "Looks as if it could withstand a storm even better than old Craggy Tops. I'll join you if a hurricane blows up!"

The four friends grinned at one another, all antagonism forgotten.

"OK," she said, as she heaved the boot open. "Let's get this shopping in before it gets dark, and I'll make us some supper – you can eat in the tent if you like. . . . Oh, and by the way, Jack and Lucy-Ann ..." she said as they all trooped into the house carrying bags of shopping. "Have you read your Uncle Eustace's letter yet?"

The cheerful smiles all immediately disappeared.

"I know you don't want to," Alison said sympathetically, "but you're going to have to read it sometime, and it might as well be now as later."

CHAPTER THREE

There was a sharp knock on the door. Sir George cleared his throat and called, "Come in, Cunningham. It's not locked."

Bill took a deep breath and pushed it open. "Here we go again," he thought. "Wonder what the Foreign Office has in store for me this time?"

Sir George gestured to the worn velvet chair on the opposite side of the table and as Bill sat, he turned the computer screen on his desk towards the young man. Bill found himself looking at a map of a familiar coastal area. "And take a look at these too," Sir George said, spreading three or four photographs out in front of him.

He cleared his throat again, and in a serious tone said, "I'm not going to lie to you, Cunningham; this is a tough mission. For the past year or so, highly toxic and dangerously unstable irradiated rods have somehow found their way into the hands of terrorists and other unscrupulous organisations. We've already lost one secret agent on this job – presumed murdered – and we don't want to lose another. That's his body in the photographs. As you can see, he was found lying face down at the water's edge. Although he didn't die from radiation poisoning, his body was chock-a-block with the stuff. We can only surmise that the source of the material lies in the area he'd designated for further investigation."

Sir George tapped a command into the computer. The image of a large white house, set in spectacular isolation between an area of wooded hills and the coast, flickered on to the screen. It was perched atop high white cliffs. Beyond these, nothing but the restless ocean for as far as the eye could see.

Bill started with surprise. "But that's—"

"Yes," said Sir George gravely. "Mrs Mannering's house."

"And the agent was killed there?" Bill asked in shocked disbelief.

"No, we don't think so. Had the forensics crawling all over the place last week. Convinced the locals they were geologists looking for evidence of ancient volcanic activity! They think the body was either dumped there or may have washed down through one of the underground streams in the area."

Bill let out a small but perceptible sigh of relief.

Sir George raised his eyebrows and smiled. "She's very pretty, isn't she – Mrs Mannering?"

"Yes, I suppose so," said Bill cautiously.

"I expect it's time you paid her a visit. Hmm?"

For a few moments Bill looked rather puzzled. "Oh, I see!" he said, suddenly realising what he was being asked to do.

"Naturally, this is all highly confidential, Cunningham. Mrs Mannering – and everyone else for that matter – must be kept completely ignorant of the real reason for your visit."

"Yes, sir."

The two men stood up. "Well, get cracking," said Sir George amiably. "You're young, she's young. There's a telephone. Wangle yourself an invite!"

"Boo-hoo! Boo-hoo!" wailed Kiki, waggling her head from side to side. She was perched on the piano's music stand, peering over Jack and Lucy-Ann's heads. They were sitting next to one another on the piano stool. Philip and Dinah leant against the instrument's side, listening to Jack as he read aloud his uncle's dreaded letter.

> ". . . I can't say I want to return from America at this moment. In fact, the timing is most inconvenient. I have a substantial amount of work still to do here and will be forced to abandon it entirely if I leave now. And quite irrespective of this, I'm feeling exhausted and somewhat under the weather. However, your holidays will soon be over, and I cannot possibly impose upon Mrs Mannering's good nature and hospitality by leaving you there any longer. I will be arriving in the UK on Friday. Please be packed and ready to come home on Saturday. I shall ring to discuss your travel arrangements with Mrs Mannering.
> Aunty Steph sends her regards.
> Yours, Uncle Eustace."

Jack stopped reading, and for a few moments the children stared at one another in forlorn silence.

"He sounds almost as keen to see you as you are to see him!" joked Philip.

"Yes, I'm afraid so," said Jack despondently.

"I don't want to go home. I'm happy here," said Lucy-Ann quietly, tears welling in her eyes.

"Me too," agreed Jack.

"Why don't you just tell him you want to stay here with us then?" suggested Dinah.

Philip banged his fist excitedly on the piano top. It boomed with a deep resonance as if to give power to the suggestion.

"Brilliant idea, Dinah! That's it! Just tell him straight. You don't want to, and are not going to go back to him!" Philip beamed triumphantly.

"But how can we do that?" asked Jack, not at all convinced by Philip's enthusiasm.

Philip thought for a moment. "We could get Mum to talk to him. She'd tell him what a good idea it would be."

Dinah agreed and, pulling Philip out of the room, said, "Come on, Philip. Let's ask her now."

Tears trickled silently down Lucy-Ann's cheeks.

"Please don't cry, Lucy-Ann," said Jack, putting a comforting arm round his sister's shoulder.

She sniffed dejectedly and, almost in a whisper, said, "I wish Mummy and Daddy were still alive."

"I know. So do I." Jack gave her a squeeze. "But they're not."

They were both quiet for a moment, then Jack pulled himself together. "It's no good wishing for the impossible," he said. "We must be sensible about this. The next best thing would be to stay here with Philip and Dinah." He began to pick out a desultory tune on the piano. Lucy-Ann slammed her hands down on the keys in frustration and anger. A horrible discordant noise reverberated around the room as the two sad children looked helplessly at one another.

Philip and Dinah burst into the kitchen and skidded to a halt. Their mother peered over the fridge door at them.

"Mum . . ." began Philip, not quite sure how best to phrase his request.

"Yes?"

Dinah butted in and breathlessly explained the whole sorry story.

"Look, you two, I know he's a difficult man, but he's still their uncle – their guardian –" said Alison. "I don't like having to say this, any more than they want to do it, but Jack and Lucy-Ann are just going to have to go back to him. They, and you, must understand that."

"Couldn't we adopt them?" said Philip wildly.

"Oh Philip! Do be sensible," said his mother, with an edge of exasperation creeping into her voice.

"But we could, couldn't we?" he demanded.

Dinah chimed in, "Oh please Mum! Can we?"

"I'm sorry," she said firmly. "It's not that simple. You're just going to have to forget that idea. All right?" she said sternly.

"Yeah, OK," said Philip morosely. He and Dinah walked slowly and sadly out of the kitchen.

CHAPTER FOUR

The full moon hung in the inky black sky above Woods Castle.

An old woman, her face anxious and care-worn, slowly climbed a winding staircase. To light her way she held before her a three-pronged candelabra.

At last she reached the uppermost floor and stopped to draw breath before venturing into the dark room. The only sound was that of rasping breathing coming from the furthest corner. The old woman tiptoed quietly towards the bed there and gazed tenderly at the face of the sleeper. A dark hood covered his forehead and the candlelight threw the rest of his pale face into deep shadowy pits and hollows.

But the old woman did not seem afraid. She stroked his hand with infinite gentleness, and whispered with heart-breaking sorrow in her voice, "Oh Gary . . . my darling boy . . ."

As Gary slept on in the turret room at the top of the castle, another man worked way below in its depths.

Bright sat in front of a long panel of computers and video monitors. He was a tall, elegantly dressed man in his late forties. His eyes were as steely grey as his temper was vicious. Never without a bag of jelly babies, he now popped a green one into his mouth to aid his concentration. At his fingertips a control and monitoring console flickered and bleeped. He leant forward intently, staring at one of the screens.

He was watching two men, working deep beneath the castle in a secret cavern. Both were clad from top to toe in white protective overalls with visored helmets, and heavy-looking boots and gloves. Slowly and methodically, they were loading a trolley with heavy metal rods. When at last it was full they pushed it from the loading bay along a rail track towards an eerily lit passage.

By the time they reached the chamber at the end of the passage, and despite their dark visors, the men were forced to shield their eyes with one hand. The sickly green light was now so intensely bright it was almost unbearable. The craggy walls all round glowed with an unearthly luminosity. The men knew only too well that exposure to it could cost them their lives. Now, munching coolly on a red jelly baby, even Bright, watching from the safety of his computer room, had to slip on the dark glasses that he always kept handy in his breast pocket.

At the end of the rail track lay a deadly radiation pool. Flames licked and scuttled across its surface and the vapours rising from it were searingly hot. The workers, with infinite care but working faster now, fixed the trolley to the lever that would tip their heavy cargo into this evil pool.

Bright smiled quietly to himself.

On the furthest screen, he suddenly noticed a group of workers clustered around a radiation monitor. They appeared to be arguing. Bright swiftly checked the corresponding radiation reading on his monitor and realised the men were alarmed by the flashing red warning light.

Seconds later, a blinding white flash filled not only the chamber, but the entire adjoining cavern. The console screamed and red warning lights flashed as its radiation sensors shot into overload.

Bright quickly flicked a switch and spoke

into a microphone. His authoritative voice boomed into the loading bay. The workers turned to listen to their employer.

"Look, I've told you before, it's perfectly safe. That monitor has a failing circuit and can't be relied on. It always gives inaccurate measurements. I have a completely clear reading up here. You are in absolutely no danger," he lied. "Besides, even if it were accurate, you're wearing state-of-the-art protective clothing . . . Now, get a move on. You've wasted enough time already. The quicker we get this job finished, the sooner we can get out of this madhouse, and the richer we'll all be."

After a moment's hesitation the men seemed to accept Bright's reassurance. They obediently returned to their loading crates. But the monitor continued to flash ominously and persistently as they passed.

"What a fabulous moon," said Jack, who was leaning mournfully against the tent pole looking out over the Craggy Tops garden. Behind him, a Gaz lamp lit a game of chess. Kiki, on a perch in the corner, seemed as depressed as the children.

Philip tried to explain. "Mum's very

24

sorry, you know, but she just can't do anything about it . . ."

"Yes, well, I didn't think she could . . . not really." said Jack. Philip felt awful. As if he were somehow partly to blame.

"Oh, I so wish we could stay here with you," burst out Lucy-Ann.

This, of course, made Philip feel even worse. "So do I, Lucy-Ann," he said, rather lamely.

"Well, we can't," said Jack firmly. "So let's just forget about it shall we . . . Hey! I think I just heard that long-eared owl screeching. I've never seen one before. What do you say we go find it, hey? One last adventure before we have to go back to – Uncle Eustace. To boredom!"

"Can't we do it in the morning?" sighed Lucy-Ann, rubbing her eyes.

"Do it in the morning!" said Jack scathingly.

Lucy-Ann was slightly embarrassed. "Oh yeah, that's right, they go to bed then, don't they?"

"I'll come with you," said Philip, eagerly grabbing a torch.

"Me too!" said Dinah, as she unhooked the lamp.

"I'm staying here," said Lucy-Ann, with a tired yawn.

"As you like," said Jack, and added to the others as he clambered out of the tent, "Come on then. But don't make a noise, all right? I want to identify the bird, not disturb it. See you later, Lucy-gater."

Suddenly, Lucy-Ann was alone in the dimly–lit tent. She felt frightened and abandoned. "Hey, wait!" she cried, scuttling to the entrance. "You can't just leave me on my own! Wait for me, you lot," she called, dashing across the lawn to catch up with them.

CHAPTER FIVE

"Hello. Alison Mannering speaking."

"Hello, Allie. Bill Cunningham here—"

"Oh Bill! How lovely to hear from you!" Alison said, laughing into the phone.

"I hope you don't mind me calling you like this," said Bill, turning his back on Sir George, who was grinning inanely at him, "but I have a few days off work, and thought a walking holiday in your neck of the woods might be fun. I wondered if I could drop by and see you all?"

"Oh, how wonderful! You'll stay with us of course?" she said. "We have heaps of space. Uncle Joss is halfway round the world visiting old army pals, so you can have his room . . . "

"That's very sweet of you, Allie. I didn't want to put you out, but yes, of course, I'd love to stay at Craggy Tops! I'll be arriving by train tomorrow, if that's all right?"

"No trouble at all. Just give me a ring when it gets in, and I'll come and pick you up," said Alison. "The kids'll be almost as pleased to see you as I will be! They're camping out on the lawn tonight," she added. "I'll go and tell them the good news now – if they're still awake!"

Bill put the phone down looking decidedly glum. Sir George patted him on the back. "Well done, Cunningham. That walking holiday idea will be splendid cover. That and staying with the Mannerings should mean you can snoop around without anyone getting too suspicious, eh?" He chuckled, but when Bill didn't answer, asked, "Anything wrong?"

Bill confessed he hated having to deceive Alison.

Sir George was only mildly sympathetic. "I'm afraid you have to resign yourself to it, old boy. Deception's all part and parcel of the job, y'know. Women, Cunningham, are a complication that you can ill afford – you'll find they always interfere with the job."

Mrs Brimming was closing the black-out curtains when Bright came briskly into the kitchen. He sniffed the air appreciatively, but didn't thank her when she placed a steaming plate of dinner before him.

"Good Heavens, woman! Haven't you closed those yet?" he complained angrily.

"You know how important it is that the castle appears deserted."

She didn't answer.

"Give me some more light! How can I be expected to eat in the dark?" he demanded, and gave her a venomous glare. She placed the three-pronged candelabra in the centre of the table and all four corners of the kitchen fell into deep shadow. Neither of them noticed Gary's dark, hooded figure glide to a stop in the doorway.

"How's the work proceeding?" she asked, when Bright had stuffed an enormous forkful of food into his mouth, and was chewing vigorously.

"We're catching up," he snapped, a spray of cheese sauce sprinkling his beard. "No thanks to that weirdo son of yours. By the way, where is he?"

"He's not well. He's sleeping," she said quietly.

"Not well?" Bright scoffed, nearly choking on another mouthful. "The boy's mad, woman, not just a little bit sick. He's a first-class menace."

"I couldn't do that," she said wearily. "But I think he needs help. Yes, I admit he needs help. Goodness only knows I've tried, but he refuses to leave the castle. He just won't listen."

Bright fixed the old woman with his strange grey eyes. In a frighteningly cool voice, he said, "You just make sure you keep him under control from now on. We can't afford any more foul-ups like that hiker. Any more incidents and Gary will be receiving baptism by fire too."

"No, no!" implored the old woman, and she began desperately trying to explain her son's odd behaviour. "He wasn't always like this, Mr Bright. It was only after poor Margaret, his sister, died in a fire. They were so close . . . always playing games together. He's always blamed himself because he couldn't save her. He was so badly burnt, trying to rescue—"

"Yes, yes, Mrs Brimming." Bright was unmoved. He stood up impatiently, scraping the chair noisily along the flagstones. Then leant menacingly towards her. "Look, old woman, I have no time to listen to pathetic excuses. You just better make sure you keep him out of my sight – or else!" He marched towards the door but before he reached it he turned round and in a commanding voice said, "In fact, you should lock him in his room."

Mrs Brimming's hand flew to her cheek, and she shook her head piteously. "He'd probably jump out of the window."

Bright turned on his heels. "Best thing that could happen to him," he snarled, and was gone.

He did not see the dark shadow that slipped away from the door and went quickly down the corridor ahead of him.

CHAPTER SIX

Though the moon was full, it was still very dark beneath the trees, and the children kept close together. Jack, with an ear cocked for another screech of the owl, led the way through the nearby woods.

"We should have told your mother where we were going," whispered Lucy-Ann, who was clutching Dinah's jacket and trying to think of persuasive arguments for turning back. There really was something horribly sinister about the moon-bathed landscape.

"Hey!" hissed Jack, suddenly coming to an abrupt halt.

"What?" gasped Philip, bumping into him.

"Oh no, what is it?" moaned Dinah, hardly daring to look.

Lucy-Ann was speechless with fear, and rammed her face into Dinah's back.

"Over there, look. A sign!"

"A sign!" Enormous relief swept through his companions.

"Gosh, Jack. Don't do that!" they all chorused.

"What?" he said innocently. "Point?"

"No! Stop suddenly like that, and hiss as if you'd seen a vampire or something. Honestly, we all thought we were goners for sure."

"Sorry," said Jack, and grinned apologetically.

They turned their attention to the sign.

"*Woods Castle*," read Lucy-Ann. "*Keep Out. Building Unsafe*."

The four children stared at one another. Philip looked as if he were trying to remember something.

"Oh yes!" he exclaimed, "I heard Mum talking about it the other day. Apparently it's been abandoned for years."

"I'm amazed we haven't come across it before now," said Dinah, rubbing a nettle sting.

"I'm not," said Jack. "This sign's not very obvious from the road, and it's so overgrown I doubt many people even see the sign, let alone the wall, and presumably the castle is completely obscured by the woods."

"Come on," said Philip, keen to investigate, "let's climb over the wall. We may be able to see the castle from the other side."

"Good idea," agreed Jack. "Look, it's crumbled away just there, we can probably get a good foothold."

He and Philip waded through the nettles and began to clamber up through the gap.

"I'm not going in there," whimpered Lucy-Ann.

"I don't want to either," declared Dinah. But in no time at all both had decided it would be better to stay with the boys than to be left behind.

Soon, all four of them were perched on top of the wall. In the distance a strange, lonely-looking castle loomed above the treetops. It stood silhouetted against the silvery moon, and looked black and forbidding.

"I think it's haunted," said Lucy-Ann.

Jack rolled his eyes.

"Doesn't look haunted to me," Philip pronounced, with an assurance he didn't feel in the least.

"Oh, for goodness sake! What do you think *haunted* looks like?" Dinah demanded.

Philip considered this for a moment, then announced, "Dark and gloomy."

"Well, that castle looks decidedly *bright*

and *cheery* to me, how about you?" she said sarcastically.

"Lightning flashing, thunderbolts flying," said Jack dramatically, widening his eyes in mock terror. Philip grinned, grateful for his friend's support.

"Owls hooting," he said, following Jack's example.

"The door creaks open!" intoned Jack in a hushed voice, "and there stands . . ." He paused for dramatic effect. "MY UNCLE!"

They all laughed. But it was somewhat strained.

"Hey, look!" Philip suddenly exclaimed. "There's a light in one of the windows! Someone's in there!"

"Is it a ghost?" croaked Lucy-Ann, trembling all over now.

"Of course not." Philip dismissed the idea. "Ghosts don't need light."

"And you're the expert on ghosts, aren't you?" mocked Dinah.

Philip ignored this jibe and, getting ready to jump, said, "Come on, this really is worth investigating."

The others hesitated, not at all sure it was such a good idea.

Suddenly, out of the corner of her eye,

Dinah thought she saw something moving in the overgrown garden below. For a few seconds it hovered on her peripheral vision. Something or someone cloaked in black with a pale oval face and eyes that glinted in the moonlight. She couldn't help it. Dinah opened her mouth and let out a blood-curdling scream.

CHAPTER SEVEN

Philip, Jack and Lucy-Ann almost fell off the wall in shock.

"What is it, Dinah?"

"What did you see?"

"Was it a ghost?" they all demanded at once, breathless with fear, and staring wild-eyed about them.

"I saw . . . I saw . . . I saw something . . . horrible," gulped Dinah, taking deep, fast breaths, "Something not . . . not . . . human."

"I knew it!" wailed Lucy-Ann. "I told you, didn't I? A ghost!"

"There's no such thing as ghosts," said Philip firmly, as much to convince himself as Lucy-Ann and the others.

"I really think we should go home now," said Lucy Ann in a shaky voice. She'd had quite enough surprises for one night.

Alison couldn't wait to tell the children that Bill was coming the next day. She tiptoed across the lawn and, quiet as a mouse, lifted the entrance flap. She started back in surprise. The tent was empty! A small, miserable squawk alerted her to the perch in the far corner.

"Hello, Kiki," she said gently, feeling instantly reassured that the children must be somewhere nearby. "Have those monsters gone inside and left you alone? Come with me. We'll soon find them," she cooed, lifting the bird from its perch.

But the children were nowhere to be seen or heard. With every unanswered call, Alison grew increasingly anxious.

"Philip! . . . Dinah! . . . Jack and Lucy-Ann! Where are you?" she shouted as she searched every room. She even rushed out on to the lawn and peered into the murky moonlit night.

"Children!" she called loudly, cupping her hands to her mouth. "Children! If you're out there, will you please come in! Now! This instant. Please!"

There was no reply.

Alison's heart was thumping. What if something dreadful had happened? She turned and ran back towards the house, her mind in turmoil about what to do next. Just as she reached the door, she looked over her shoulder one more time. The children raced round the corner, apparently out of nowhere. They were upon her in a panting heap before she could even breathe a sigh of relief.

"Where have you *been*?" she demanded.

"Looking for a long-eared owl," said Jack, as they all shuffled thankfully into the brightly lit house.

"Well, I was just about to phone the police."

"Why?" asked Dinah, genuinely surprised.

"WHY?!" Alison was amazed. "Because I'd assumed you were all safe in the tent. What was I supposed to think when I came out to tell you something, only to find a solitary parrot and not one of you in sight? And now you tell me you've been roaming in the woods, hunting for some bird!"

"Long-eared owl! They're terribly rare, you know," Jack piped up helpfully.

"Right! That's it! I've had enough!" said Alison, her panic and relief turning into irritation. "Upstairs, all of you! That's the end of the tent for tonight. Go on, go to bed," she commanded, waving them upstairs.

The four children filed past her feeling suitably chastised. Each of them mumbled a sheepish and heartfelt apology as they passed. Philip was the last. He turned to face Alison.

"We really are sorry, Mum," he said quietly.

Alison melted a little. "So you should be," she said. "Please, don't ever do anything like that again." She stroked Philip's cheek affectionately and smiled. "We'll say no more about it. Now, off you go."

She watched him clomp up the stairs after the others. When he'd almost reached the top, a thought occurred to him, and he paused mid-step.

"Mum, do you know anything about Woods Castle?" he asked.

"Why do you want to know?" she asked curiously.

"We could see it from a wall near the woods," Philip admitted.

Alison raised her eyebrows. "Could you indeed! Well, the only thing I do know is that it's structurally unsafe. So you lot keep away from it, do you hear?"

"Yes, Mum. Goodnight. And sorry for upsetting you," he said. "We didn't mean to."

"Goodnight, sweetie, sleep tight," she

answered warmly.

"What's that infernal noise?" wondered Bright angrily, as he passed the closed doors of the great hall. It was after midnight and he had at last completed his final inspection of the day. After yet another altercation with the men working in the cavern, he was feeling exhausted and intensely irritable.

He paused outside the room. Dust drifted silently in the rich golden light that filtered through the keyhole into the dimly lit corridor. Light seeping under the doorway glazed the caps of his shoes. They glowed like molten rock as he pressed an ear to the wood. The latticed ironwork was refreshingly cool against his aching head. He closed his eyes and listened. The murmuring sound was still not loud enough to identify. Bright cautiously turned the handle and opened the door.

The room was illuminated by hundreds of candles. Some stood in simple candleholders, others in jars or in dripping pools of congealing wax. Two enormous candle chandeliers hung from the ceiling and still more lined the walls.

Bright saw before him the back of the

familiar hooded figure.

Gary was kneeling before the gigantic fireplace, his face uplifted to the portrait of a young woman. By turns, he flung his hands wide, then wrung them in desperate prayer. From his mouth there flowed a babble of words and strange incantations.

Bright strained to make sense of the chant.

"Save us . . . unbelievers . . . Evil . . ."

It was impossible to understand. Bright shook his head contemptuously, and quietly withdrew.

"At least I know where the madman is," he muttered to himself.

CHAPTER EIGHT

"Oh, Bill, there's a breathtaking view over the valley here. Shall we stop?"

Alison pulled over to the verge and she and Bill climbed out of the car to admire the scene. Below them, Craggy Tops lay gleaming white and peaceful and the blue sea glinted in the sun.

Bill drew in his breath with pleasure. "It's beautiful," he said, turning to Alison. "You and the kids are very lucky."

"Mmm," she agreed, nodding her head happily, "I think you're right."

Bill turned to survey the scene once more. He shaded his eyes with both hands and squinted into the sun.

"I'm glad you're on holiday this time. You work far too hard, Bill," Alison said, smiling at him.

"Yes . . ." he said hesitantly, and frowned.

Alison noticed a troubled expression flicker across his face and gave him a gentle prod. "Whatever it is exactly that you do!" she teased.

Bill smiled. "Oh, just the same old stuff, Allie," he said blithely, as if it were of no interest whatsoever.

Alison studied his face for a moment. Then she smiled broadly and said, "It's not all bad though, is it? If it hadn't been for the adventure on the Isle of Gloom over there," she said, pointing into the far distance, "we'd never have been lucky enough to meet you!"

"Very true, Allie!" he said, and they both laughed.

"Come on, mystery man," she said warmly, "let's get back to the kids. They're dying to see you."

"Greedy pig! Greedy pig!" chanted Kiki.

Philip glared at the traitor on his shoulder. He quickly snapped the box of chocolates shut and hid it behind his back. He, Jack and Lucy-Ann all attempted to look innocently employed as Alison bustled past. But she seemed to have a sixth sense about such things.

"Oy! Kiki's right! Chocolates *after* lunch, you lot," she scolded.

"No chocolates for you – you treacherous bird-brain," said Philip. "Bread and water only, for traitors . . ." he said dramatically.

"I'm just going to cut a few herbs," said

Alison as she went out to the garden. "Can you set the table for lunch please?"

As the door closed behind her mother, Dinah skidded breathlessly into the room.

"I think Bill has his gun with him!" she whispered excitedly. "I'm pretty sure I saw him putting it in a drawer just now, when I went upstairs to tell him lunch was almost ready."

"You must have imagined it," said Philip, trying to think of a reasonable explanation.

"He wouldn't need a gun on holiday, surely?" said Lucy-Ann.

"Maybe," suggested Jack, his eyes lighting up, "he's not on holiday!"

The four children looked at one another in a stunned and thoughtful silence.

"Sshh," hissed Dinah suddenly.

Alison was halfway through the door. "Ah, Bill, there you are! Come in and sit down," she said, as he stepped into the kitchen through the doorway opposite. "By the way, children, I hope you thanked Bill for the wonderful chocolates," she said, fixing them with her eyes.

"They certainly did!" exclaimed Bill, grinning at their eager faces. "Positively swamped me in gratitude!"

"Let's eat! Let's eat!" squawked Kiki.

"Good idea," said Alison. "It's all ready now."

After a couple of mouthfuls, Philip said boldly, "I wish you were investigating a mystery, Bill. We could help you!"

"Sorry to disappoint you, Philip, but I'm just on holiday," Bill said without batting an eyelid.

"Do you have your gun with you?" asked Lucy-Ann sweetly.

Bill shifted uneasily in his chair and looked at her curiously. "No," he said slowly, "Of course not, I'm—"

"For heaven's sake, children," Alison interrupted. "Stop giving Bill the third degree and leave the poor man in peace. He's on holiday. So let him enjoy it!"

After lunch, Alison shooed the children on to the veranda with the box of chocolates. "Don't eat them all at once, or you'll be sick." She tickled Kiki under the chin indulgently. "Sick as parrots!" she joked.

"Let's go and investigate Woods Castle," suggested Jack, as he popped a chocolate into Kiki's beak and selected another for himself.

"Good idea," agreed Philip, stuffing three chocolates into his mouth at the same time.

"Yeah," huffed Dinah who was performing a particularly spectacular handstand against the wall, "Let's leave Mum and Bill on their own for a bit."

The others turned towards her.

"Well, he's awfully nice, isn't he?" she said, reddening a little. But whether it was because her matchmaking was so obvious, or simply a result of her prolonged handstand, it was difficult to say.

"I don't want to go to the castle," muttered Lucy-Ann. Then more firmly she said, "It's too scary. Couldn't we do something else?"

"Oh come on, Lucy-Ann." Jack tried hard to enthuse her. "It won't be frightening in daylight. Besides, it's the last chance we'll have for an adventure before we go back to Uncle Eustace," he added dejectedly.

But, no matter what the others said to persuade her it would be fun, Lucy-Ann remained unconvinced.

"Stay at home then," said Jack irritably, fed up to have wasted so much time. "But don't you dare tell Allie where we've gone. She'd be livid."

"I'm not going to lie!" said Lucy-Ann, outraged. "Oh, all right then," she said grudgingly, deciding it was the lesser of two evils, "I'll come."

Philip jumped up. "Come on, let's go," he urged, eager for a new adventure.

As the children trooped past, Philip slipped the box of chocolates through the kitchen window. "See you later, Mum," he called. "We're just going for a walk in the woods."

They were almost out of earshot by the time Alison had stuck her head out the window.

"Be careful!" she called.

Mrs Brimming, out of breath from the climb, held a tray of food in one hand. She tapped on her son's bedroom door with the other.

"Gary?" she said softly, but there was no reply. She knocked again, but there was still no answer. She pushed the door open and entered the room. It was empty.

"Oh, no!" she wailed, and rushed anxiously to the window. He was nowhere in sight.

CHAPTER NINE

"Here goes then," said Philip grandly. "This is a huge step for mankind, and I'm the man to take it. Louis Armstrong would be proud of me." He took a bow.

"Neil Armstrong, you twit," corrected Dinah, giving him a shove to the top of the tumbledown wall.

With a bit of heaving and pushing, all four of them were soon standing in the castle grounds. Dinah was pressing a soothing dock leaf to the nettle sting on her elbow.

"Help! I've never seen so many stingy and scratchy things. Perhaps this wasn't such a good idea after all."

"Don't be such a sissy. Come on," said Philip, who'd just then found a long, stout stick that would be perfect for swathing through the nettles and brambles. "This way I think . . ." and he plunged forward, following, if he did but know it, the same route that the hiker had taken only a week before.

Dinah, Jack and Lucy-Ann followed, grateful for the path Philip was clearing for them. Kiki flew between the children as they walked, occasionally alighting on Jack's shoulder screeching. "Hurry up, slow coach!"

It was a beautiful day. Insects and birds buzzed and flittered about them. Crickets sang in the high grasses. It was all so calm – so normal – the children began to think they'd been foolish to imagine anything strange lurked in the castle and its grounds. None of them noticed the figure that tracked their progress with a curious intensity. It stalked silently alongside them, just out of earshot. Its long, dark wool clothing was a perfect camouflage.

When the brambles ended abruptly, the children found themselves in a cool woodland glade. The light breeze shifted the dappled shadows gently about them and the landscape rippled under a kaleidoscopic mixture of delicious greens and browns.

"Gosh, isn't it beautiful!" said Lucy-Ann quietly, completely forgetting her reluctance to be there at all.

Philip was still up ahead. They ran to catch up with him and he spun round at the sound of their approach.

"On guard!" he cried, lunging forward with one hand on his hip and the other outstretched holding the stick before him.

"Oh, do shut up, Philip," said Dinah, laughing.

"I was just thinking," said Philip, as he tucked the stick through his belt so that it hung at his side like a sword in its scabbard, "that if the worst came to the worst, you two could always hide in the castle!"

Jack and Lucy-Ann looked dubious, then Jack perked up.

"Sanctuary, you mean?"

"Absolutely!" grinned Philip.

"But you're only given sanctuary in a church," remarked Lucy-Ann.

"A castle's almost a church," said Philip, trying to rescue another of his brilliant ideas.

"Yes! And we could bring food and water to you every day," said Dinah, enthusiastically.

"Every day would be an adventure!" beamed Philip.

"But what would happen when you and Dinah went back to school?" It was Jack's turn to point out a flaw in the idea.

Philip and Dinah looked crestfallen. "Oh dear, forgot about that," they said apologetically, sorry to have dashed their friends' hopes.

The children walked on, each absorbed in their own thoughts. The woodland opened out on to a lake and following the overgrown path that skirted around its edge, the children discovered themselves staring up at the castle.

"Heavens!" gulped Dinah, "I had no idea we were so close!"

"Yes, here it is," said Alison, pulling the map from the drawer. She joined Bill at the kitchen table, and spread it out.

"Let's see," she said. "I haven't actually had any time to do any walking myself, so I'm not sure what to recommend."

Bill pointed to a small symbol. "What's this? A castle?" he asked conversationally to conceal his special interest in it.

Alison bent down to inspect the map more closely. "Yes, I think it's in the woods not far from here. Apparently it's been empty for years. Local gossip has it that it's haunted," she said, smiling.

CHAPTER TEN

Up close, the castle looked even more menacing than the children had imagined. All four felt suddenly chilled to the marrow as they huddled together nervously, surveying it with a peculiar mixture of curiosity, awe and fear.

The great blocks of stone from which it was constructed were dark with age and speckled with sombre-coloured lichens. Grotesque gargoyles protruded at regular intervals around the battlements. Others sprouted from above the mean turret windows, their hideous faces twisted into ugly grimaces.

Here and there, the castle was covered in thick, dark green, waxy vines. Their spidery tendrils crept like aliens up the wall, finding their way into even the smallest crevices.

"It's just like a castle under some grim enchantment in an old fairy tale," said Dinah, her hushed voice breaking the silence.

"Come on," said Jack, gathering courage and nudging the others into action. "Let's take a closer look."

The castle looked as ominous as ever, but still not one sound disturbed its implacable façade. They looked at one another in silent agreement. It was now or never.

They climbed the steps.

Two stone lions roared silently on their pedestals on either side of the entrance. The children stepped forward—

CRACK!

They froze, almost petrified with fear, then spun round and stared wildly about them. Kiki gave a startled squawk and flew to the safety of a broken window ledge high above.

The children saw nothing move but a speckled bird on the steps below. It had been holding a snail in its beak, and it too had taken off in sudden fright.

"It must have been that thrush trying to crack the snail's shell!" said Jack, grinning with relief.

Lucy-Ann wasn't the slightest convinced by this explanation, and hung on even more tightly to Jack's arm.

He turned his attention back to the castle in search of Kiki.

"There you are, you stupid bird. Come here," Jack cooed when he spotted her on the ledge outside a broken window. He pulled a few fluff-covered sunflower seeds from his pocket and tried in vain to entice her down.

"I don't like it here," moaned Lucy-Ann, trembling violently, "I want to go home."

Her fear was infectious.

"What's the matter?" asked Philip, trying to sound as if he wasn't in the least bothered by the unexplained noise and the eerie atmosphere.

CRACK!

It was even louder this time. And nearer! They all whirled round.

"Who's out there?" shrieked Dinah.

Lucy-Ann was backing down the steps, white-faced with horror. Then she ran – as fast as her legs could carry her.

"Wait for me, Lucy-Ann, I'm coming too!" screamed Dinah, leaping down the steps two at a time. The boys gave a regretful look at Kiki, then fled, hot on the girls' heels.

The woods seemed dense and endless. They reverberated with the sound of the children's frantic footsteps and rasping breath.

The sound of heavier feet than theirs

pounded fast and close behind them.

"Something's following us!" screamed Dinah, but they were all so intent upon reaching the gap in the wall that none dared to look back.

They burst into the sunlit area at the edge of the overgrown garden.

The heavy footsteps suddenly ceased but the children didn't stop to wonder why. They leapt through the scrub and bramble, and almost cleared the wall in a single bound, so desperate were they to get away.

In various states of collapse, they slowly recovered their breath.

"What," gasped Philip, "were we running from?"

"I don't know," panted Jack, bent double and clutching a stitch in his side.

"We heard a noise," said Dinah.

"We ran because we heard a measly noise?!" rasped Philip.

"We ran because we were frightened!" Lucy-Ann stated with straightforward clarity.

"Of what?" asked Philip.

There was a pause.

"A . . . an animal?" suggested Dinah uncertainly.

"A bull? A horse? A cow? What?" persisted Philip.

Dinah thought for a moment.

"Well," she said, "it was big."

Jack looked suddenly ashen. "Kiki!" he muttered in despair.

"No, Gary, no!" Mrs Brimming had cried, holding her hands defensively in front of her body to block Gary's path as he hurtled through the trees after the fleeing children. His eyes blazed with excitement, and insane laughter gurgled in his throat as she caught him roughly by the arm. She gripped him with all her strength as he struggled to continue the chase.

"They're only children! Please, Gary! It's enough just to frighten them," she pleaded, staggering in the struggle to hold him back. The sound of the running children faded rapidly into the distance. Only when they could no longer be heard did Gary grow suddenly calm. He stared vacantly at his mother as if waiting for instruction.

"Good boy, Gary," she said in a soothing voice, and taking his arm she led him slowly back to the castle.

"Naughty boy! Naughty boy!" screeched

Kiki as they came into view.

Startled by the raucous scolding, Gary looked up. Sitting on the window ledge of his room was the pretty white parrot he had seen flitting about the children in the woods earlier. Gary's eyes glittered beneath his hood, and a quiet smile lit his face.

CHAPTER ELEVEN

"Mum! Bill!" Philip rushed headlong into the kitchen at Craggy Tops.

Alison and Bill looked up from the map, startled by his sudden appearance.

"Philip! Whatever's the matter? Are you all right? . . . And where are the others?" demanded Alison, looking past him into the empty hall.

Philip, who'd run the entire way without stopping, flopped into a chair and caught his breath for a moment.

"I left them at the castle!" he gasped.

Alison looked at him in disbelief.

"I told you not to go there," she said, gripping his shoulders. Then, holding him at arms length, she looked anxiously into his face. "Are the others hurt? Who's hurt, Philip?"

"No, no!" said Philip, as if this were a preposterous idea. "It's not that. It's Kiki!"

Alison let go of him and straightened up. She looked bewildered.

"What about Kiki?" she asked.

"She's lost! Somewhere in the castle!" he wailed.

Alison, feeling mightily relieved, put a comforting arm round him. "Oh, is that all!" she said, ruffling his hair affectionately, and smiling at Bill.

"But we have to find her, Mum!" Philip cried. "We didn't want to go in the castle by ourselves. Couldn't Bill come with us, and help look for her?" he pleaded, turning to their friend.

"Yes, of course I will. Lead the way!" said Bill, without a moment's hesitation.

"I'll drive you," said Philip's mother. "I'll just get the keys. Meet you outside."

As they hurried out to the car, Bill turned to Philip.

"Are you all right?" he asked urgently. Philip was surprised by his tone of voice.

"Yes. Why do you ask?" he said suspiciously.

"You look as if you'd seen a ghost or something, that's all," Bill said, watching Philip closely.

Philip gulped and managed a strangled laugh. "I've just been running hard," he said, "and, you know, worried about Kiki."

Bill didn't look at all convinced.

The others rushed up to meet the car as it

bounced up the pot-holed road.

"Still no sign of Kiki," said Jack miserably as he, Dinah and Lucy-Ann clambered into the back.

"Don't worry, Jack," said Alison, smiling at him in the rear-view mirror, "we'll find her."

She turned off the track on to the castle drive, and soon they were drawing up in front of the castle itself. The children tumbled out of the car, and began to call Kiki's name.

"What was that?" whispered Mrs Brimming. She rushed to the window and peered through the broken glass. "It's those children again! And two adults! Getting out of a car!" She pressed a gnarled hand to her throat. "We're done for, Gary," she moaned quietly.

A low, amused chuckle came from behind her and she turned to face her son. The white parrot was perched on Gary's arm and he was caressing it with infinite tenderness. The bird crooned with contented pleasure.

"Oh, Gary," she said, slowly shaking her head. "What are we going to do?" She wrung her hands in wretched uncertainty. "It's no good, I'll have to tell Mr Bright." She pulled Gary firmly but gently to the bed. "Now, stay here, and don't let them see you," she instructed. She hurried quickly from the room in search of Bright.

When she'd gone, Gary rose and carefully placed the parrot in a rusting, dome-shaped bird cage. He hooked his fingers through the small looped handle at the top and glided silently to the window.

He watched as Bill and Alison joined the children in front of the castle door. Their cries were clearly audible.

"Kiki! Kiki! Where are you? Kiki! Come on, Kiki. Look . . . chocolate!"

Sudden realisation flickered across Gary's face. "Ahh! Kiki!" he cooed. He stared into the cage and chuckled with delight. His eyes glowed. "Kiki!" he said, stroking the wire bars. "Kiki!"

"Wipe your feet!" shrilled Kiki. "Naughty boy!"

Gary stared at the bird in surprise, then carried it quickly to the bed and draped a folded blanket over the cage.

"Turn on the light!" came Kiki's outraged scream, muffled now. "Turn on the light!"

Gary picked up the cage and slipped quietly down the stairs.

"Turn on the light! Naughty boy!" screeched Kiki, her voice echoing down the spiral staircase.

"What a monstrous carbuncle of a building," mused Bill, as he surveyed the massive structure before them. Then, shrugging his shoulders, he returned to the business at hand. "Now, Jack, stop shouting and tell us exactly where you last saw Kiki."

As Jack pointed to the broken window above, Alison pointed meaningfully at a warning sign nailed to the castle door. She turned Philip to face it. "You see!" she said, "KEEP OUT. BUILDING UNSAFE!" To emphasise the point, she tapped each of the words as she read them.

"But we didn't go *in* the castle, Mum," protested Philip.

Alison put her hands on her hips. "You shouldn't have been here at all," she reprimanded. "And please don't pretend that you thought otherwise."

Lucy-Ann touched her arm. "We didn't mean any harm, Allie."

Alison looked down at her for a moment,

then gave her an affectionate and forgiving hug. "I know you didn't, sweetie, but that's exactly how you find yourself in all these pickles, isn't it?"

"Right!" interrupted Bill. "How about tackling this problem with a little military discipline? Allie and I'll do a recce round the back and you—"

It was Alison's turn to interrupt. "You lot will stay right here!" She pointed to the front step beneath them. "And wait for us. Understood?" she said firmly, looking at each of them in turn.

"Yes, Mum," said Dinah, clicking her heels together and giving Alison an obedient salute.

"I mean it, Dinah!" said her mother sternly, pointing an authoritative finger at her.

Mrs Brimming hurriedly drew the thick black-lined kitchen curtains so not a glimmer of light shone through. She felt weak and her body trembled. She leant heavily against the sink.

"How many, woman?" Bright demanded belligerently from behind her.

"Two adults and four children," she said,

turning to face him. "I think it may have been their bird that Gary found. Perhaps they've come to look for it?" Bright stared furiously at her.

"What shall we do?" she asked, her hands fluttering about in distress.

"Nothing," he hissed. "As far as they're concerned, the castle's deserted. They'll soon discover there's no way in and give up. There's nothing to worry about."

He paced up and down without speaking, then suddenly snapped his head up. "Unless," he said in a low voice, "that feeble-minded, maniac son of yours decides to attack them, that is."

CHAPTER TWELVE

"I'm scared," said Lucy-Ann, huddling closer to Dinah and Philip. "Can't we go round the back with Allie and Bill?"

The three of them were leaning against one of the stone lions. Jack was lounging dejectedly against the castle door.

"No," said Dinah, "Mum said we should stay put. Just keep an eye out for Kiki—"

"Wipe your feet!" There was a faint but familiar screech.

Jack bounded forward, his body tense with excitement. "Sshh! Listen!" he hissed, straining to hear something.

Philip stood up. "What is it, Jack?"

Jack waved his hands frantically to silence him, and put a finger to his lips.

The four children listened intently. "Naughty boy!" They were rewarded with another distant screech. It seemed to come from somewhere inside the castle.

"Kiki!" exclaimed Jack. "It's Kiki!"

They all rushed to the castle door, and pressed their ears to it.

"She's definitely inside," said Philip. "But how on earth are we going to get in?"

He put his shoulder to the wood and pushed as hard as he could.

"It'll never give," said Jack, pulling him away. "We'll have to find another way." He dashed down the steps and began searching round the side of the castle they had not yet investigated.

"We'd better tell Allie and Bill," said Lucy-Ann.

"Don't be silly!" exclaimed Philip. He stepped back and scanned the front of the castle once more. "If only we could reach that broken window," he said regretfully.

"Well, we can't, bird-brain," said Dinah, giving him a rap on the forehead.

"Oh yes we can!" yelled Jack, as he appeared round the corner. "Come and help me. I've found an old ladder!"

The others rushed over, half expecting it to be a joke. But there, lying in the grass, was indeed a ladder! It had obviously been there for a long time. Grass and brambles had grown through and over it to such an extent that it was almost completely hidden beneath the vegetation.

"Phew, it's a bit rickety!" huffed Philip, as they all levered it up and propped it against the wall for inspection.

"I must say," said Dinah, more than a little dubious, "it doesn't look especially strong."

"It looks fine for our purposes," said Jack. Nothing was going to stop him getting into the castle to get Kiki back.

So they all heaved the ladder to the spot beneath the broken window and leant it carefully against the ledge.

Philip, who was the heaviest, elected himself the first to climb.

"Now, hold it steady," he said, and cautiously trod the first rung. It creaked a little, but held firm. He gingerly tested the next. It too held, and drawing courage from this, he began to climb faster. He reached the ledge without mishap and hauled himself through the broken pane. He disappeared from sight as the others stared up at the window open-mouthed. But a moment later he poked his head out and called, "Come on, it's all right, I'll hold the ladder."

Dinah was next. Secure in the assumption that if the ladder was sturdy enough to withstand her brother's weight, it would easily support her own, she was shocked when the first rung cracked and splintered beneath her foot. She screamed in surprise. But with Philip coaxing from above, she slowly continued the ascent and reached the window safely.

"Come on, Lucy-Ann, now you." Jack held the ladder steady from below as Lucy-Ann stepped carefully up the rungs. She gripped the sides tightly and dared not look down. Dinah and Philip hauled her into the window at the top.

"You now, Jack. Up the beanstalk!" joked Philip.

Jack grinned up at them, and slowly began to climb. Midway up, the ladder began to groan and shudder alarmingly. The three children held their breath as they watched Jack's precarious progress.

Philip leant as far out of the window as he could, his arm stretched down to grasp his friend as soon as he came into reach.

C-R-A-A-A-C-K!

Just as he neared the top, the rung beneath Jack's foot splintered and gave way. The ladder began to slew frighteningly out of control. He reached wildly for Philip's outstretched hand and just managed to catch it as the ladder dropped away. He gripped his friend's hand for dear life as Philip and Dinah hauled him up the wall on to the ledge and into the room.

The four children stood breathless for a moment, too shocked to speak.

"Phew! That was close!" said Dinah, letting out a sigh of relief.

"No it wasn't. You were holding me," said Jack, trying to convince himself he'd been in no real danger.

"Mmm," said Dinah, without much conviction.

Horrified that she might have lost her precious brother, Lucy-Ann gripped his arm tightly as if she'd never let him go.

"Come on," said Jack, prising her off and taking stock of their surroundings, "we have to find Kiki. That's what we're here for, isn't it?"

They all looked around the turret room. It was dark and gloomy and furnished only with a single bed. Kiki certainly wasn't there.

"Look – a spiral staircase," called Philip. "Let's see where it leads."

The others followed cautiously as he led the way down.

"Do you think anyone actually lives here?" murmured Lucy-Ann.

Dust billowed on the stairs and mice scuttled around their feet as they passed.

"Doesn't look much like it," said Jack, eyeing a particularly large mouse as it scampered into a crack in the stonework.

"But what about the lights we saw the other night?" Dinah reminded them.

They'd reached the bottom of the stairs now and were edging their way along a dank corridor.

"Sshh!" whispered Philip, and held up a hand in warning. The children had reached the end of the corridor and now stood peering over his shoulder into the gloom before them.

"It's the entrance hall!" said Philip in amazement. He'd been convinced they were heading in completely the opposite direction.

"You're right!" said Dinah, equally surprised. "Those are obviously the front doors," she said, pointing past his ear.

"Where do you suppose the other doors lead?" whispered Lucy-Ann nervously.

"Only one way to find out. Come on," said Jack, as he pushed past her.

The others followed warily. They all stopped by one of the inner doors and leant hard against the wood, straining to hear any sound of life from within. But the castle remained steadfastly silent.

"I think it's empty," whispered Philip. The others nodded their agreement as he slowly turned the handle. He peered round the edge of the door. His eyes took a few moments to adjust to the light and then he whispered, "Wow! It's like some kind of strange church!"

The others pushed him forward impatiently and shuffled in behind. They stood in the middle of the room and looked about in awe.

It was the great hall where Bright had seen Gary the previous night, chanting and praying, but now light streamed into the room through the four massive, high-arched windows. The lead lattice-work divisions chequered the floor with a pattern of criss-crossed shadows, and dust whirled quietly in the sunlight. Dominating the whole room was a large portrait of young blonde woman. It was hung above a huge and cavernous fireplace.

"Strange is not the word!" said Dinah, shivering. "It's absolutely freakish."

Suddenly, in the distance, they all heard a door slam. They stood rooted to the spot, hopelessly trying to guess which direction it had come from.

Then they heard muffled voices – coming towards them!

"Where can we hide?" said Dinah urgently, looking wildly around the room. Philip rushed to the door they had come through and peered out. But it was too late!

"A man and an old woman are coming this way!" he whispered, retreating hastily.

Jack in the meantime had found a door at the back of the room.

"Come on, in here. Quick! There's another room."

The children sprinted across the floor, and pulled the door soundlessly shut behind them.

They pressed heavily against it but could hear nothing, so turned to inspect the room.

"What do you suppose this room's for?" Jack said, spluttering somewhat. A great plume of dust had risen from a sheet as he'd lifted it to inspect the lumpy shape beneath.

Everything was swathed in cobwebs. Shelves lined every wall from floor to ceiling with nothing more than layer upon layer of dust to support.

"Dunno," said Philip, tracing a finger through the grime. "Looks like it was once a library."

Lucy-Ann felt her hair stand on end and goose pimples rise on her arms. "What a horrible-looking man," she said, her voice trembling.

The others turned to gaze at the portrait she was staring at. Dinah stood on tiptoe and read the name written on the frame. "The Reverend Doctor Brimming."

Suddenly, a low tremulous musical note filled the room and then, just as abruptly, it stopped with a discordant plunk. The children whirled round.

"What was that?" said Philip, gulping.

"I don't know," said Jack, peering cautiously under another dust sheet.

"Sounded a bit like an organ . . ." said Dinah. "It's all just too creepy."

They were sure they were alone in the room, yet each of them was equally certain that the sound had come from within it.

Lucy-Ann, terrified, began to moan. She tugged pleadingly at Jack's arm. "I want to get out. There's something in here . . . something vile . . . I can feel it . . ." Then with a sharp intake of breath she dug her fingernails into Jack's arm. "Look!" she gasped.

CHAPTER THIRTEEN

"I'm taking no chances, old woman," said Bright acidly, tucking a small revolver into his waistband. "We have too much to lose."

Mrs Brimming shuffled along beside him as he headed towards the computer room. For every one of his steps, she took two. Every now and again she gave him a sideways glance, as if trying to gauge the best moment to speak.

"Shipment must be ready by end of week . . . those slackers below will just have to work an extra shift tonight. Imperative we get out of here soon as possible," he muttered under his breath, and ran a distracted hand through his hair.

Mrs Brimming chose this moment to speak.

"Is that wise?" she asked anxiously. "Gary says there's a dangerously high level of radiation in the sealed cavern . . . and I think," her voice dropped almost to a whisper, "he's been talking to the men."

Bright stopped mid-pace, and turned angrily towards her. "He's what?" he snarled, his eyes blazing. "How dare he spread alarm amongst the men! Every precaution has been taken . . . the levels are perfectly safe . . ."

Mrs Brimming held out her hands pitifully. "No, Mr Bright, please!" she begged. "I know Gary shouldn't have said anything, but please don't hurt him, please don't upset him!"

"Upset *him*!" Bright stared at her in disbelief.

Mrs Brimming trembled uncontrollably, but she stood her ground. "He seems to have calmed down a little since he found the bird. I'm terribly afraid if he's upset again, he'll—" The words choked in her throat.

Bright dug hard into his pocket and extracted a jelly baby. He now stared at her like a man possessed. He raised the sweet wordlessly to his mouth and chomped off its head with venomous and obvious meaning.

"I promise, Mr Bright," the old woman said in a frightened, high-pitched voice, "I'll take him for treatment as soon as you've paid us."

Bright swallowed the pulped jelly with a chilling grimace, then dropped his face until it was within half an inch of her own.

"Quite right," he said slowly in a low, sarcastic tone. "Now, leave me be, old woman, I have work to do!" He turned away in disgust and stomped down the corridor.

RED ALERT! READ ALERT! RADIATION ABOVE RECOMMENDED LEVEL. ALERT ALL WORKERS AND EVACUATE. ACTIVATE DECONTAMINATION PROCEDURE. DO NOT ATTEMPT ENTRY INTO CHAMBERS. TOXIC AIR. REPEAT, TOXIC AIR. RED ALERT! RED ALERT! RADIATION LEVEL ABOVE . . .

The electronic voice repeated the warning in the same urgent tone. A light pulsed in rapid accompaniment, illuminating the dark room every two seconds with a diffused red light. Bright rushed in and flung himself into a chair. He jerked a keyboard towards him and rapidly tapped a complex series of code numbers into the computer. He sat back, gripping the edge of the seat so hard that his knuckles began to turn white. He cursed Mrs Brimming for delaying his arrival at the room and scraped the chair back in great agitation. He flicked on the computer video screens to inspect the activity in the secret cavern. All was as he'd hoped. No one had yet noticed the red light flashing on the wall monitor.

CAUTION!

Bright whipped his head back to the computer.

YOU HAVE OVER-RIDDEN THE RADIATION LEVEL METER. PLEASE CHECK YOUR INSTRUCTIONS AND CONFIRM COMMAND. REPEAT, CONFIRM COMMAND. CAUTION!

Bright flung himself forward, and tapped in a confirmation code.

CODE ACCEPTED. OVERRIDE COMPLETE IN FIVE SECONDS. FIVE, FOUR, THREE, TWO . . .

Bright rubbed his hands together in satisfaction and peered once more at the video screens. Two workers stumbled heavily in their unwieldy protective boots as they pushed an empty trolley back towards the loading bay. Bright smiled to himself as he watched one of them approach the monitor. A green light flickered above its dial. The man tapped it doubtfully, but the meter continued to read a steady SAFE. This seemed to satisfy the man and he turned to give his mate a reassuring thumbs up.

"You fools," hissed Bright, and his body shook with silent laughter.

CHAPTER FOURTEEN

The portrait seemed to be coming alive. Its previously blank eyes now glittered malevolently.

"It's watching—!"

But Lucy-Ann's words were drowned out by another blast of the music. And this time it didn't stop. Slowly, the intense relentless rhythm of it swelled about them into an ever-rising crescendo of sound.

"What is it?" shouted Jack, pressing his hands over his ears. But the others were doing exactly the same thing and didn't hear a single word.

With every second the music grew louder, pounding its heavy rhythm right through every bone of the children's bodies. Clutching their hands to their ears and hardly able to think, they reeled about the room desperately trying to block out the unbearable noise. The portrait's eyes glittered with manic glee as they watched how the children screamed.

The whole room seemed to swirl and judder beneath them as if the sound were rocking its very foundations. They flung themselves under the dust sheets, pressing their ears against the musty cushioning of the old chairs. Philip managed to wrap the thick drapes around his head. But nothing could protect them from the excruciating pounding of the music.

The door burst open, and Mrs Brimming bolted into the library. Her hands, too, were clamped against her ears as she rushed forward and stood trembling before the portrait.

"Gary! . . . Gary, what are you doing?" she shouted, her body shaking with despair and the pulverising sound of the music.

The portrait's eyes stared intently at her and flickered uncertainly for a few moments. Suddenly, the room was plunged into an unexpected and blissfully deafening silence.

Mrs Brimming slumped forward with overwhelming relief, and dropped her hands wearily from her ears. She looked up at the portrait as though to say something, but the eyes were now blank. She sighed deeply and began to walk slowly from the room as though she were laden with an enormous burden.

Just as she was about to close the door, a muffled sound caught her attention. She looked curiously back into the room. The dust sheet over one of the armchairs shivered and muttered. Mrs Brimming took a faltering step forward and roughly pulled the covers off the chair.

Lucy-Ann gave a cry as Mrs Brimming pulled at her. Philip staggered out from behind one of the ancient velvet curtains. Jack and Dinah began to emerge from their hiding places. They were all shaken and disorientated and did not hear the old woman's shocked exclamation of surprise and fear.

Mrs Brimming took a deep breath and began desperately to haul the children out of the room.

"Who are you? How did you get in?" she demanded as she pushed them into the main hall. She looked anxiously back at the portrait. The children were still too dazed to speak, but she didn't seem to care that they did not answer.

"Never mind that," she said urgently as she hustled them into the entrance hall. "Let's get you out of here first. Come on! Don't hang about! It's not safe! Out, out,

out!" She gave Dinah an encouraging shove. "Go on!" she insisted, looking over her shoulder nervously.

Mrs Brimming rounded them up in front of the entrance doors, and as she grappled with the lock, Lucy-Ann stooped to pick up a small white feather that lay on the ground. She slipped it into her pocket.

Bill and Alison had walked round the entire castle. Concluding it was well and truly empty, not to mention impenetrable, they now returned to the double doors at the front. The children weren't there.

"Wait till I get my hands on those—"

Alison was interrupted by a loud creaking of hinges as the big doors opened behind her. The four children and Mrs Brimming squinted into the sun for a moment but as the fuzzy shapes before them turned into Alison and Bill, the children rushed forwards. Dinah flung herself into her mother's arms and the others crowded about her, all speaking at once.

Mrs Brimming stepped forward. "Do these children belong to you?" she demanded.

"Yes, they do," said Alison, trying to extract herself from the grip of eight hands and four clamouring voices. "I'm terribly sorry. What have they been up to?"

Mrs Brimming glared at her.

"This is private property!" she reminded them. "You must have seen the sign?"

Everyone nodded rather sheepishly, but it was Alison who apologised.

Mrs Brimming's face softened a fraction and her voice was more normal and under control when next she spoke.

"I'm sorry I was so rough with them but the castle is structurally extremely dangerous – as these children very nearly discovered to their cost. I've lived here all my life and there are places even I won't go."

"We just had a bit of a fright, that's all," said Dinah, attempting to reassure Alison.

Obviously extremely agitated, Mrs Brimming glanced over her shoulder and turned hastily back to the intruders.

"Well, it's done now," she said dismissively and began to heave one of the doors closed. "The important thing is that no one was hurt." She looked up with a start. "What brought you here in the first place?" she asked sharply.

Bill who had been watching her closely spoke for the first time. "We're looking for the boy's lost parrot."

Mrs Brimming hesitated for a moment and her eyes slid guiltily away from their faces. She looked into the distance as she spoke. "I've not seen hide nor feather of a bird," she said firmly.

"Well, she was here," said Jack with equal firmness.

Mrs Brimming glared at him.

"Is there anyone else here who might have seen it?" asked Bill, being ultra-charming and polite.

"No," she snapped, again looking nervously over her shoulder. "I live here on my own." She began to reach for the second door.

Alison stepped forward with her hand outstretched. "Well, I do apologise if the children have caused any trouble, Mrs—?"

"Brimming," the old woman said sharply and ignored the proffered hand.

"We've taken up quite enough of Mrs Brimming's time, you lot. Come on, let's go," said Alison and began herding the children towards the car.

Bill lingered behind to ask a few more questions of the old lady.

"So you've lived here all your life?" he enquired, lounging conversationally on the closed door.

"Yes," said Mrs Brimming passionately. "And my mother and father before me and their parents before them. And my boy was born here. He's—" The animation drained rapidly from her voice. "He's a scientist . . . at the university," she said quietly.

Bill stepped away from the doors a little and looked up at the decaying façade. "It's a fine old place. Pity it's been allowed to get so run down," he said.

Mrs Brimming could barely disguise the bitterness in her voice. "I couldn't agree more. But it would take millions to restore it."

A beep on the car horn at that moment, prompted Bill to take his leave. "Ah, I'm summoned! Thanks very much for your time. Goodbye, Mrs Brimming."

She gave him a curt nod and stood in the doorway until the Land Rover was out of sight. Then she turned and walked back into the castle, slamming the door shut behind her.

CHAPTER FIFTEEN

"Don't worry, I'll meet the deadline . . . No, no problems at all . . ." Bright paced up and down the kitchen, speaking into a mobile phone. Every now and again he dipped into his pocket and drew out a jelly baby. He stared thoughtfully at each one before popping it into his mouth. Suddenly, he laughed derisively into the mouthpiece. "Witnesses? There'll be no witnesses! If the radiation doesn't see to it, rest assured, I shall!"

He cut his laugh short as Mrs Brimming appeared at the kitchen doorway.

"Must go. 'Bye," Bright snapped and hurriedly turned off the phone. He pulled a chair out and sat in it heavily. He regarded Mrs Brimming with silent irritation for a moment and then indicated with a terse flick of his head that she should sit opposite him.

"Oh, that was close!" she said with a sigh and lowered herself gratefully on to the chair. "I was so afraid Gary would suddenly appear."

Bright held up his hand commandingly.

"Look, we have people prepared to pay us very good money for those irradiated rods. That's all that concerns me. Now, old woman, I intend to speak to that mad son of yours."

Mrs Brimming looked anxious. "Oh, please, no, not now . . . he's terribly overwrought!" she begged. But Bright would not be persuaded. He thumped the table and leant forward aggressively. "Listen, the last thing we need is the police on our backs. He needs to be told – and told today. I insist that you take me to him at once!"

Mrs Brimming was too exhausted and too afraid to defy him. With a heavy heart, she rose slowly from the table and led Bright in search of her son.

When the two of them entered the turret room they found Gary trying to force the caged bird to eat a nut. He whistled softly at the parrot but it refused to accept the food.

"Jack! Jack! Jack!" Kiki squawked miserably. "Oh, save me!"

Mrs Brimming placed her hands gently on Gary's shoulders. "Gary, dear, leave the poor bird in peace," she said kindly. "It's terrified." There was no response. Gary continued to offer Kiki the nut as if he were completely unaware of the presence of his mother and Bright. Mrs Brimming shook him a little and tried once more in a stiffer tone. "Gary, please! We have something very important to say to you." But he remained apparently completely oblivious of them.

Bright was becoming increasingly impatient and burst out angrily, "Gary! Are you listening?"

"Sshh! Please!" entreated Mrs Brimming. "Now, Gary dear," she said, wrapping her arms around his body and turning him gently towards Bright who had slumped on to the bed, "Listen to what Mr Bright has to say."

Gary stared down at him blankly.

"It's like talking to a brick wall. *You* keep trying to get through to the moron," said Bright, realising he was never going to get a reaction from this lunatic.

Mrs Brimming cupped Gary's chin in her hands and lifted his pale oval face to hers. In a soft voice, she began to speak.

"Gary, listen. We're so close to achieving all our dreams. You've worked so hard, for so long. You found the pool in the cavern below and discovered what to do with it. With the money we earn we can rebuild the castle. Use it as a sanctuary like you've always wanted . . ."

Gary visibly relaxed and for a moment his eyes shone.

Mrs Brimming shook him gently again and, looking intently at him, added, "That's why you must control yourself. The hiker was bad enough. But if you'd harmed those children . . ."

Both Mrs Brimming and Bright stared at Gary's stupefied face, waiting for even the slightest hint of a response.

Bright stood up. "Well?" he said. "Has he understood?"

Gary shot Bright a look of pure hatred.

"Yes, he understood all right," said Mrs Brimming quietly.

Bright was undaunted. "I hope so, for his sake. He's becoming too much of a liability. And as for that parrot—" He advanced towards the cage. "I'm going to give it back to its owners. We simply can't risk them returning—"

Before he could say another word, Bright felt himself gripped by Gary's hands and his feet lifted from the ground. Gary's eyes blazed into Bright's.

"You must say he can keep the bird. It's the only way," begged Mrs Brimming. When Bright at last gurgled a choked assent she clutched Gary's arm. "Let him go, Gary! I promise you, I won't let him take the parrot."

At last the terrible grip loosened and Bright sagged to the floor, gasping for breath. He crawled towards the door, pulled himself up and staggered from the room , followed rapidly by Mrs Brimming.

Gary turned quietly back to the cage. "Kiki!" he crooned and once again proffered the nut through the bars.

CHAPTER SIXTEEN

By the time Bright reached the last flight he was descending two steps at a time. He was boiling with rage. "He's a monster!" he bellowed as Mrs Brimming tried desperately to keep up with him.

"But he can be helped!" she cried.

Bright snorted scornfully and turned to her in disgust. "Can't you see? Are you blind, woman? He's long past help!"

Mrs Brimming's knees buckled beneath her and she sank to the ground at his feet. "Oh, please," she begged, looking up into Bright's twisted face, "just finish the job and go. Leave Gary alone . . . I'll get help for him."

Bright pushed her away and without another word he strode down the gloomy corridor out of sight, the sound of his heels clicking sharply on the flagstone floor.

"You are all to stay away from that place. Is that clear?" said Alison firmly as they drove home towards Craggy Tops. She could see Jack in the rear-view mirror. He looked thoroughly miserable.

"Oh, Jack, I do understand what you're feeling. But this just wasn't – isn't – the right way to go about finding Kiki."

"What other way is there?" he asked crossly.

"Kiki's good at finding her way home, Jack. She's probably waiting for you there!" said Dinah.

But none of this seemed to cheer Jack up. "Somehow I don't think that's very likely," he said, and turned to stare out the window once more.

Alison spoke again. "You'll just have to trust Mrs Brimming. I'm sure she'll find Kiki if she's there. I'm sorry, but I do mean it. You are not to go back to that castle."

Craggy Tops looked wonderfully peaceful and welcoming as the car crunched up the gravel drive. The instant they came to a halt, Jack, Dinah and Philip leapt out and raced into the house to look for the lost bird. Lucy-Ann stood stroking the feather in her pocket as she watched their frantic activity. She frowned. She had a terrible dilemma. If she told the others about the feather, Jack would be bound to return to the castle even though Alison had strictly forbidden him – them – to do so. But

93

if she didn't . . .

It was not until after dinner, when all the children were sitting on the stairs trying to make sense of what had happened, that Lucy-Ann finally decided to confess.

"Where did you find it?" demanded Jack in surprise as he snatched the feather from her fingers. He looked at her keenly.

Lucy-Ann shuffled her feet uneasily and then in a little voice admitted, "In the castle. By the front door."

"Right!" said Jack, now knowing what he had to do. "The feather clinches it. I'm going back." He stood up and began to trudge up the stairs.

"But Jack, you can't," cried Dinah, "Not after what happened – that awful noise. And besides, Mum—"

"I'm not going back to Uncle's without Kiki," Jack stated categorically, his knuckles whitening as he gripped the banister.

Philip, who had been pondering the matter all through dinner, now attempted to give a reasonable explanation for the mysterious noise.

"It could have been an alarm of some sort," he suggested, swivelling round to watch Jack's reaction.

But a mere alarm wasn't going to put Jack off.

"So, I've just got to be careful," he said and stomped up to his room.

The others turned to face one another.

Lucy-Ann looked worried. "And what about the eyes?" she said.

Philip tried to brush this fear aside. "We could've imagined that. The noise – the alarm probably confused us—"

"It did not! And anyway, how could we all imagine exactly the same thing?" Lucy-Ann said indignantly.

Just then, Jack popped his head over the top of the banisters. "I don't care about the stupid noise or the stupid eyes. I'm going back and that's final!" He stomped off to his room.

CHAPTER SEVENTEEN

It was dusk at Craggy Tops. Bill paced to and fro on the lawn, speaking in a low voice into his mobile phone.

"I've discovered an interesting castle, Sir George. It's in a secluded wood nearby. It was supposed to be uninhabited, but, er," Bill paused, and switched the mobile phone to his other ear, "turns out there's an old lady living there . . . I don't know. But I'm sure something strange is going on. Yes sir, I'm taking another look at it tomorrow . . ." Bill spotted Alison coming towards him across the grass. "Must go. 'Bye, sir," he said hastily, and turned off the phone just as she reached him.

"Secrets?" she asked, smiling at him.

"Er . . . the reception's rather poor in the house," he explained.

Alison couldn't help noticing his slight hesitation and looked at him curiously. "You could have used our phone, Bill."

He looked back at the house and in a joking tone said, "Thanks. I know, but I thought I'd let the department pay!"

"I thought you were on holiday?" she

probed, only half joking.

"I am!" said Bill, smiling broadly to dispel any doubts. "But I just had to check up on a little unfinished business."

"Mmm." Alison gave him a quizzical look. "I don't know that I like your business," she said.

Bill hooked his arm through hers and began to propel her gently towards the house. "I don't like it much myself sometimes," he said, "but it's not worth dwelling on." His voice became buoyant. "Come on, Allie, it's getting dark. Let's go and cheer Jack up. He seems terribly upset about Kiki."

"Hmm," she murmured thoughtfully. Not for the first time, she had seen how eager he was to turn the conversation away from his job.

"Poor Jack," said Allie. "That bird's so important to him, Bill. Not just as a pet. Apart from Lucy-Ann, Kiki's all he has left of his first family. If he loses her . . ." her voice trailed off.

Bill looked concerned. "Yes—" he began, but Alison was so absorbed in her train of thought that she didn't really hear him.

"It wouldn't be so bad if their uncle wanted them. But of course he doesn't." She looked sadly into Bill's eyes. "He just feels they're a burden."

"I can't imagine why," said Bill thoughtfully. "I mean, I know two children are a huge responsibility but they seem exceptionally nice kids."

Alison smiled. "Aren't they just? And they get on so well with Philip and Dinah. They even asked me to adopt Jack and Lucy-Ann the other day, but . . ." she stared into space.

"That's one answer. Could you?" Bill asked.

"Oh, I'd do it all right. Like a shot," said Alison. "But how on earth would I go about it? And much as he doesn't want them himself, I'm sure their uncle wouldn't be willing."

"Allie, seriously, if adoption's too complicated, you could always apply to be their legal guardian."

"What a brilliant idea, Bill! I hadn't thought of that. I'll certainly check it out." Alison beamed, glad to have Bill around to talk to.

*

Night had fallen. Gary crept down the stairs to the great hall. He carried the caged Kiki in one hand and felt his way through the gloom with the other. He breathed deeply when at last he closed the hall doors behind him. He quickly drew the curtains. Then he began methodically to light every candle in the room. When at last he'd finished, it blazed with glorious flickering light. He placed Kiki's cage on the floor before the portrait of the young woman and drew ten fresh candles from a hidden pocket. These he placed in a lighted circle around the cage. As he stood to admire his work, he stumbled and fell. The hood that perpetually covered his head slipped back to reveal his face. Although he was a young man in his late twenties, his face was frighteningly haggard and drawn. An ugly red scar mottled his forehead and the side of his face. He immediately scooped up the hood and crouched forward, peering into the bird cage.

"You won't leave me, will you?" he whispered. "I can take care of you . . ." He stroked the bars and smiled sadly at the parrot. A tear welled in his eye and ran silently down his cheek. Kiki cocked her head on one side, eyed him uncertainly, and let out a startled squawk when Gary suddenly leapt up. He raised his arms and spread them wide, his head held high in exaltation as he faced the portrait. His eyes blazed wildly in the guttering candlelight as he launched into a mad sermonising.

"I am the guardian. I am the guardian of history. The guardian of this castle. I am the guardian of all mankind." He dropped heavily to his knees, though his face remained uplifted and his arms outstretched. "From the ruins of this castle shall spring forth a new castle. It will provide shelter for the saved. A haven for . . ."

Kiki rocked back and forth uneasily but Gary was oblivious to her distress. ". . . while outside the sinful world is consumed by diabolical flames," he cried, his face rapturous with his own crazed vision of the future.

As good as his word, Jack had set off when he was sure the others had fallen asleep. He now hurried through the moonlit woods towards the castle. Looped across his chest and over his shoulder, he carried a thick rope, and in his hand, a torch.

It was rather more scary than he'd imagined, being alone in the woods. Every shadow unnerved him and the slightest noise made his heart beat thunderously. He wanted to turn and run back to the safety of Craggy Tops but the thought of Kiki lost and alone spurred him on.

CHAPTER EIGHTEEN

Philip woke with a start and sat bolt upright in bed.

"Jack?" he whispered, turning in the dark towards the other bed. "Are you awake?" There was no reply. Philip leant over, fumbled for the bedside lamp and switched it on. He stared at Jack's rumpled bed. It was empty!

"Oh, no! The idiot's gone to the castle!" he said, slapping the palm of his hand against his forehead in consternation. He leapt out of bed and hurriedly pulled on some clothes over his pyjamas. He grabbed his torch, and crept along the hall to Dinah and Lucy-Ann's room. He slipped in, switched on the light, and began to whisper, "Hey, you two . . ."

Philip couldn't believe it. Their beds were empty too!

"They wouldn't have gone without me, surely?" he thought as he tiptoed downstairs, puzzled but also feeling rather hurt.

As he crept towards the kitchen he heard stifled giggles. He pushed open the kitchen door and shone his torch into the room. The beam hit Lucy-Ann first and then Dinah. Both girls looked up with startled, guilty expressions. They were sitting at the table, each in front of a large bowl of apple pie, ice-cream and lashings of chocolate sauce.

"There you are!" whispered Philip, pinging on the main light. "Where's Jack?"

"Isn't he with you?" They giggled and resumed tucking into their dessert.

"No, he isn't. I'm sure he's gone to look for Kiki."

"Oh, no!" Dinah's laden spoon dropped from her mouth. "Mum'll be furious!"

"I know. He's being completely stupid," said Philip, scooping a dollop of ice-cream out of her bowl with his finger.

Lucy-Ann looked worried. "What are we going to do?" she asked.

"We'll have to go after him. Before he gets into trouble . . . and before Mum finds out."

"Come on, Lucy-Ann," said Dinah, grabbing her friend's arm. "We'll go and get dressed. Wait here, Philip, we'll be back in a jiffy."

Philip sat down in front of the abandoned feast. But Dinah and Lucy-Ann were back before he'd had even two decent mouthfuls.

All three of them were soon running at full pelt towards the dark woods. The girls caught up with Philip at the castle wall and they all clambered over breathlessly.

"Come on, stick close and follow me," said Philip, leading the way forward with his torch.

The girls hastened after him again, stumbling over hidden roots and stones.

"Philip, please slow down," wailed Dinah. "It may be a full moon, but it's still pretty black under these trees. It's all right for you, you have a torch, but if you keep whizzing off, Lucy-Ann and I can't see where we're—"

"Blast!" K-PLAGH!

"Dinah? You all right?" asked Philip, scanning the woodland floor with his torch. It spotlit Dinah's face as she lifted her nose from the ground.

She glared up at him. "I think I'll live!" she hissed. "No thanks to you."

Philip and Lucy-Ann hauled her up and grinned at her while she rubbed her knees and elbows.

"What are you two Cheshires grinning at?" she said with dignity and marched forward. "Come on."

Jack reached the steps leading up to the castle, and stopped. He listened intently for a few moments but heard nothing except the hoot of a distant barn owl. He moved towards the window he and the others had climbed through the day before, unwinding the rope and tying one end round the middle of a strong stick he'd selected specifically for the purpose. He took a few steps back and peered up. It was higher than he'd thought, but he was sure he could do it. He took a deep breath and held the stick to his shoulder like a javelin. He took aim, and drew his arm back.

A cold hand gripped his wrist! He was so startled that he neither exclaimed nor moved.

"Don't be stupid!" said a familiar voice behind him.

Jack exhaled an enormous sigh of relief. "Philip!" he whispered and then added with some irritation, "Let go! Leave me alone!" Jack tried to wriggle his wrist free.

"But it'll never work, Jack. We have to find an easier way in."

Dinah and Lucy-Ann arrived, panting and out of breath, just in time to agree with

Philip. Jack glared at them.

"Look, I'm not leaving Kiki behind!" he said defiantly and shook his hand free.

Philip walked towards the corner of the castle.

"Of course we won't leave her behind," he said. "But we have to find her together. Come on, let's see if we can find a way in round the back. Bill and Mum might have missed something."

Jack silently conceded that Philip and the others were probably talking sense, and he loped after him. Dinah and Lucy-Ann followed close behind.

As Alison and Bill had discovered before them, it was difficult to walk around. Creepers, scrubby bushes and weeds grew high up the walls and tall nettles grew in great patches everywhere.

"Sshh!" hissed Philip suddenly. "I heard voices and . . . look!"

The others followed the direction of his finger. A chink of light gleamed through the curtains of a window on the ground floor.

"It's ajar!" whispered Jack excitedly.

Bent double, he crept up and crouched beneath it. He ushered the others to his side, and when they were all safely lined up under the sill, they listened for a moment to the low murmur that issued from the room. Then, very slowly, Jack lifted his head and peered through the gap.

"It's a kitchen," he whispered to the others. "Mrs Brimming's talking to a man who's . . . Sshh!"

Jack suddenly ducked down and the children pressed themselves flat against the cold stone wall.

"What is it?" Philip hissed, fearing that Jack had been spotted.

"They're leaving the room!" grinned Jack. "Hang on, I'll just check." He raised himself briefly, then gave the all-clear. "They're gone."

The children looked at one another.

"Shall we give it a try then?" said Philip.

"They might come back," whispered Dinah, voicing the fear no one else dared to utter.

"I'm going to risk it anyway," whispered Jack and within seconds the window was open and he'd pulled himself on to the ledge. Philip needed no encouragement to follow.

"We must be crazy!" said Dinah to Lucy-Ann as they too pulled themselves through the window.

Crash! An horrendously loud sound splintered the air. Jack and Philip spun round.

"Eek! Sorry! Didn't mean to – knocked a cup and saucer off," whispered Dinah as she jumped to the kitchen floor.

"Somebody's coming!" rasped Jack, who'd heard footsteps approaching down the corridor. Horror spread across their faces. Lucy-Ann, who was still climbing through the window on to the draining board, was absolutely terror-stricken. They all looked desperately about the room for somewhere to hide.

CHAPTER NINETEEN

"The Apocalypse approaches like a dark cloud on the horizon. There is not long to wait now . . ." Gary cried, his wailing chant growing wilder and more fanatical by the minute. ". . . Searing sin from the face of the earth."

He still knelt on the floor and swayed violently from side to side as he spoke. His face was radiant as he addressed the portrait. "Margaret, oh Margaret . . . only those who have embraced The Way will be granted salvation . . ."

Kiki, trapped in her caged ring of fire, listened nervously to the madman's proclamations. "Poor old Kiki! Poor old Kiki!" she bawled and rattled the bars frantically.

"Under here!" whispered Dinah, and as one, they flung themselves under the table.

They were just in time. Within seconds, Bright entered the room. The children huddled together as tightly as they could, thankful for the long tablecloth and the dark shadow it cast around them. Hardly daring to breathe, they watched the man's feet from beneath the table as he passed along its length towards the window. They heard the tap being turned on, then off.

Suddenly, Bright's hand appeared beneath the tablecloth. Jack stifled the scream that was bursting to get out of Lucy-Ann's mouth, and gripped her tightly.

"Hello, puss," said Bright, in a gentle voice, and stroked the large tabby cat that sat by one of the table legs. None of the children had noticed it sitting there, just inches away from them.

After tickling it under the chin, Bright rose. He stood for a moment in silent contemplation. The children stared at his shoes, willing him to leave. To their infinite relief, he began to walk towards the door. But the children stiffened instantly as they saw him pause. Had he heard them? He turned! He walked quickly back to the table! This was it! He was going to lift the cloth! But no! He merely scooped up a large slice of chocolate cake from the table. The children watched him leave the room. As he turned into the gloomy corridor they caught a glimpse of a smile as he stuffed the cake greedily into his mouth.

"Phew!" breathed Dinah when they were sure he was gone for good. "That was pretty close!"

Jack was impatient. They'd wasted enough time already. "Come on," he said, easing himself out into the light. "We've got to get a move on or we'll never find Kiki."

The others slithered out after him, and they all crept warily into the corridor.

It was dark, but some distance ahead they could see an eerie blue light spilling out through a doorway. They tiptoed, one behind the other until they reached it. Jack peered round the corner into the room and, seeing it was empty, entered.

A wide worktop lined the entire length of one of the walls. And on this rested six computers. Each had a video screen attachment though at the moment they were all black and lifeless. The glowing blue light came from the computer screens themselves, and it was by this light alone that the room was lit.

The others watched from the doorway as Jack slid into a chair in front of the computers. He thought for a moment and then pulled a keyboard towards him.

"Come on, Jack," hissed Philip. "You said

it yourself – we haven't got all night." He looked anxiously down the corridor as Jack began to punch the keys.

"Just a minute, just trying to access some infor—"

"Jack! This is no time to be playing with computers! Come on!" whispered Lucy-Ann urgently. Jack held up his arm to quieten her. The screen fizzed with a mass of information, and then stabilised on a set of tables and figures. Jack leant forward, and read haltingly, "Uranium count . . . something to do with radiation—"

"Come on, Jack!" grumbled Philip.

"Just a minute – this could be very important," said Jack, staring intently at the screen. But almost immediately he whipped round to look at the others. They stared at him in surprise. "Didn't you hear that?" he asked in amazement.

"What?" they all said together, a blank look on their faces.

"A squawk!" croaked Jack, leaping up from the chair. "Kiki's squawk!" He rushed into the hall and ran to the end of the corridor. He stopped and peered out. The others clustered behind him.

"It's the main entrance hall again!"

whispered Philip. "We've approached it from the other side this time!"

"Sshh!" Jack whispered and led them stealthily to the doors of the great hall. They drifted behind him like ghosts, not making a sound. Jack eased the door open just a crack and gazed through it into the room.

"He's blowing out the candles. Ahh! And he has Kiki!"

"Who has?" murmured Lucy-Ann.

Jack opened the door a fraction more and Lucy-Ann stuck her nose round.

"Him!" said Jack, standing aside for Dinah to have a look too. Lucy-Ann turned round before Dinah had time to step up. "Too late. He's gone," she said. "And he's taken Kiki with him!"

"What!" thundered Jack, his voice echoing round the hall. He pushed the door wide open and ran in. The room was empty!

"He can't just have disappeared!" Dinah said in amazement after Philip had checked the adjoining library room.

"Look!" exclaimed Lucy-Ann, holding aloft another white feather. "I think he went through there," she said, pointing to the enormous fireplace. "I thought I saw something moving in it when I looked round the door, but I wasn't sure."

Jack lost no time in examining the fireplace. It was quite large enough for a man to stand upright in, and it accommodated the four children with ease.

"What exactly are we looking for?" asked Dinah, as she peered into its darkest recesses.

"Oh, well, I don't know what exactly," Jack replied, "but a lever or a handle of some sort. Or a stone that moves when it's pushed."

"Well, there's no lever," said Philip, who'd examined every square inch, "so let's try pushing all the stones."

As he spoke, Lucy-Ann pressed one of the decorative studs. She jumped and gave a squeal of surprise when it responded to her touch.

"This one moves! Look!" she gasped.

They all stared in astonishment as the entire fireplace and grate slid silently backwards to reveal a dark passage.

CHAPTER TWENTY

"Did you hear your precious son raving like a lunatic again?"

Mrs Brimming jumped at the unexpected sound of Bright's voice behind her. She didn't turn round, but continued to replace the spent candles in the candelabra.

"Yes, but he's stopped now," she said quietly.

"Where is he? In his room?" he demanded brutishly.

Mrs Brimming's hands trembled and her voice dropped to a whisper. "No . . ."

Bright strode up to her. "Well, where is he, then?" he said stridently, pulling a candle roughly out of her hand. He could see she was very nervous and far more anxious than usual as she slowly shook her head.

"You're lying," he snarled and as he saw her eyes flick towards the fireplace he raged at the poor woman. "I told you he mustn't go down there," he thundered, "under any circumstances!"

"But I can't stop him," she cried.

Bright strode to the fireplace. He pressed

the decorative stud and turned to face Mrs Brimming. "Well, I will!" he said, and ducked into the passageway.

"No, no!" cried Mrs Brimming, wringing her hands and hurrying after him. "Wait! Please! Don't upset him! He's dangerous!"

"Well," said Jack boldly, squaring his shoulders and moving determinedly towards the opening, "if Kiki's in there, I'm following." He stretched out his arm and flicked on his torch. It emitted the dimmest of light.

"Blast!" he said, shaking the wretched thing, "I knew I should have put in new batteries." He turned to Philip. "Can I borrow yours?"

Philip reached for his back pocket. "Uh oh!" he said, in a heavy voice, "I must have dropped it when we ducked under the table!"

"Great," said Dinah. "We're in the middle of a dark castle, in the middle of dark woods, in the middle of a dark night . . . without a torch! How could you drop it, you dim-wit?"

Philip looked a bit sheepish. "Sorry," he said mildly, and shrugged his shoulders.

"Too bad!" said Jack, "I'm going in." He groped his way forward, feeling the wall as a guide.

"Jack!" called Lucy-Ann plaintively as the dark entrance engulfed him.

"We can't let him go on his own," said Philip, deciding for the three of them. "Come on!"

As he ducked his head under the arch Philip noticed a lever sticking out of the wall. He waited until Lucy-Ann and Dinah had passed and then pushed it upwards. As he'd expected, it activated the closing mechanism. The fireplace slid shut as silently as it had opened.

Now that they were actually in the passage it wasn't as dark as it had first seemed. At widely spaced intervals, dim light bulbs threw just enough light for them to pick their way cautiously along the narrow tunnel.

"Jack – wait!" called Philip. His voice sounded dead and muted in the damp, confining atmosphere.

Jack paused and waited until they'd caught up, and then strode on. The passage bent sharply to the right and, as he turned into it, Jack noticed a control panel of some sort set into the wall. He stopped and studied it for a moment before turning to the others.

"That must be the back of the Reverend's portrait. Look, there are two eye holes," he said.

"I think you're right," Dinah said, and scrambled on to the inset ledge. She peered through the holes. "Yep. It's the library all right."

"Hey, look!" said Lucy-Ann. She'd just spotted a tape deck at the far end of the ledge. "That must be what whoever it was used to play that awful music . . . that noise."

Jack quickly lost interest. His one absorbing intention was to rescue Kiki. He pressed forward. "Come on!"

The passage travelled downhill steeply and every now and again twisted to the right or left. It was dank and chilly and smelt revolting.

"We've been going for ages," whispered Dinah, thinking they were never going to get out again.

"Well, it must lead somewhere!" said Jack, not for one moment losing momentum.

"Eurghh!" Dinah gasped with horror and disgust. Jack turned to check on her.

"What's the matter?"

"Spider's web!" she said, her voice hoarse with fear. It clung to her hair and was draped over her forehead. Lucy-Ann brushed it quickly away.

Dinah shuddered. "I don't mind rats and mice, but I can't stand spiders."

"Listen!" said Lucy-Ann, hyper-alert to the slightest sound. "Someone's behind us."

She was right. Voices were approaching from the same direction they had come. Philip indicated a door up ahead, and the children raced up to it. Philip wrenched it open and all four of them tumbled in, just as Bright and Mrs Brimming emerged around the corner. Philip felt for the handle on the inside of the door so that he could close it, but couldn't find one. He pulled it to as far as he was able, and they all held their breath.

"What fool left this door open?" said Bright angrily, and slammed it shut as he passed. Philip stood on tiptoe and, gripping the metal grille at the top of the door, peered out into the passage as the two people disappeared from sight.

"What now?" whispered Dinah.

"We follow them. They may lead us to Kiki," said Jack.

"I don't want to worry you, but that may not be so easy," said Philip, turning to them.

"Why not?" asked Lucy-Ann. "We only have to follow the tunnel."

"The door's shut from the other side," Philip said.

Lucy-Ann looked blank.

Philip rattled the grille in explanation. "This is a dungeon, you know. There's no handle on this side. We're trapped!"

CHAPTER TWENTY-ONE

"Push it," suggested Dinah.

"I've tried," groaned Philip. "Any other bright ideas?"

Lucy-Ann piped up. "I'm the smallest, maybe I can fit my hand through. Lift me, Philip."

He hoisted her up and she slipped her hand through the bars.

"It's no good," she said at last. "I can't reach."

They really were trapped! They plonked themselves down on the various wooden crates that were stacked about in the room.

"If only we had something to break the grille with," said Lucy-Ann in despair.

"What do you think is in these boxes?" Philip said as he stood up to examine one. Dinah tried to open it but it was locked. Philip tried more of the boxes until he eventually found one with a loose lock. He gave it a good hard kick, then bent down eagerly to prise open the lid. The others clustered round.

"Looks like a load of iron bars!" said Dinah in astonishment.

Philip grinned. "Talk about luck!"

But just as he was about to lift one out, Jack's commanding "NO!" arrested his movement. They turned to look at him.

"That stuff I saw on the computer. It was about irradiating iron bars!" Jack warned.

The others looked dismayed and stepped back from the box.

"Wouldn't they have that yellow and black danger sign on the box?" said Philip hopefully.

Jack was more pessimistic. "Maybe, maybe not," he said slowly.

"Well, if they're radioactive, the sooner we get out of here the better," said Dinah, shuddering.

Jack stooped to the box and gingerly lifted out a rod. "I got you into this mess . . ." he said as he carried it towards the door. He began to bash it against the metal grille and little by little it gave way. At last the gap was wide enough for him to slip his arm through. He groped for the handle on the other side and flipped it down. The door swung open and the others leapt forward.

"Well done, Jack!" congratulated Philip.

"Yeah, but let's get out of here," Jack said, and laid the rod carefully back in the box.

They stepped cautiously into the passage.

"Oh, no!" groaned Dinah.

Footsteps were now approaching from the other direction! They all looked round wildly. Jack darted forward and opened another door a little further down the passage.

"Quick! In here!"

The children raced down the tunnel and crammed themselves through.

This tunnel was even more poorly lit than the one they'd left, and obviously rarely used. The walls were hewn from rougher stone and were disconcertingly moist to the touch. Rubble and dust lay strewn underfoot and enormous spider webs billowed gently around their faces.

"This tunnel may lead to the same place as the other one," said Jack.

"It's probably a lot safer too," said Philip, considering the options.

The children exchanged glances, but Dinah could contain her horror no longer. "I refuse to go down here."

"Come on, Dinah," said Philip, gently taking her arm. "We really don't have any other choice."

"No! One spider's bad enough, but this ..."

The others could hear the rising panic in her voice. Philip pulled her forward. She twisted away from him but was struck dumb with horror when a thick veil of web flapped on to her face.

"It's all right, Dinah," soothed Lucy-Ann as she picked the web carefully from her friend's head.

Dinah sagged, panting and close to tears. "Is it all gone?" she gasped and added, "That's it, I'm going back!"

"Not by yourself you're not," said Philip, grabbing her arm.

"Don't worry, Dinah," said Lucy-Ann, "I'll guide you. Tie this scarf round your eyes, then you won't see."

"No!"

"It's worth a try, Dinah," urged Philip.

Dinah finally agreed, and allowed Lucy-Ann to lead her slowly along the tunnel.

"It's all right. There are no spiders near you. That's it. Come on ..."

After what seemed hours the passage suddenly twisted sharply to the right and the children found their way barred by an ancient portcullis. Beyond it, they could see a door on the right. The tunnel itself climbed upwards to the left and twisted out of sight.

Lucy-Ann peeled the scarf from Dinah's eyes as they all considered their next move.

"Hey, I wonder if this opens it!" said Lucy-Ann. She pressed a green button she'd just spotted in the wall, then she shrieked as an enormous black spider scuttled on to her hand. Without thinking, Dinah reached forward and brushed it away. They all gaped at her in amazement.

Lucy-Ann regarded her with real respect. "Wow! Thanks, Dinah!"

"Did I do that?" she said, in some astonishment herself.

A grating sound suddenly diverted their attention. The portcullis was slowly lifting.

They ducked underneath and went over to the door. It had two small, grubby glass panels set in to it. The children peered through them cautiously.

"KIKI!" exclaimed Jack.

CHAPTER TWENTY-TWO

The children were looking directly into the decontamination unit. Three workers were cowering away from Gary, who stood before them, his arms outstretched in warning. Kiki huddled in the cage at his feet.

Mrs Brimming and Bright were standing opposite. Bright was apoplectic with rage. Even from their hiding place the children could hear his shouting.

"Look, I've told you, you can't believe anything he says. He's a maniac. He's insane. It's perfectly safe in there." Bright jerked his head in the direction of the loading bay. He was incensed by the sound of Gary's soft laughter, and turned angrily towards him. "Get out of the way, you—"

Mrs Brimming stepped between them and began to plead with her son. "Gary, please listen . . . Gary—"

"Kiki," he cooed, bending to press his face to the cage and ignoring his mother. "Pretty Kiki."

Bright grabbed Mrs Brimming's arm and pulled her roughly to one side.

"Listen, old woman, that moron's putting this operation in jeopardy. If you don't keep him under control from now on, there'll be no money for you."

Mrs Brimming stared at him. "What do you mean?" she said in disbelief.

"You heard. Now, get him upstairs!" Bright's face was hideously contorted with anger.

"But he won't go without the bird," stammered Mrs Brimming. "He thinks no one can take it from him down here."

Bright whipped his head round to the three workers and clicked his fingers.

"Hold him!" he commanded. They leapt forward obediently and gripped Gary by the arms.

"Well, if he won't go, then the bird can and he'll just have to follow," snarled Bright.

But Gary hurled the workers away the instant he saw Bright pick up the cage. He lunged at him and, with his superior strength, forced him to let it go. The two men stared grimly at one another. Suddenly, Bright pulled out his gun and released the safety catch. Gary's eyes blazed with fury and before Bright could pull the trigger he had shaken the weapon from his hand. Then in one swift movement he lifted Bright from the ground and to everyone's amazement, heaved the struggling man out of the unit, through the air-lock chamber, and into the loading bay.

The workers and Mrs Brimming watched in horror. They dared not enter the contaminated cavern without taking all the necessary precautions. They turned to the large video monitors.

"No, Gary, no!" cried Mrs Brimming, as they saw him throw Bright into an empty trolley. He shoved it with all his might along the rails towards the radiation chamber.

Bright was dazed and although he tried he didn't have the strength to clamber out. A scream of agonising fear reverberated round the cavern as the trolley entered the short passage to the radiation chamber. Bright's face was illuminated for a second by the sickly green light, and then was gone.

A few moments later, the trolley shot into view on the second video screen. Everyone watched silently as it hit the side of the pool. Bright was flung violently into its noxious depths. He screamed as he entered the boiling surface. Then, soundlessly, he sank from sight.

Gary swayed over the birdcage moaning, "Kiki, Kiki . . . Kiki, Kiki . . ." over and over again. Mrs Brimming clasped his shoulders and stared vacantly into space, not knowing what to do.

The children watched the three workers edge past the hooded figure. Suddenly, Gary leapt up with a roar and grabbed one of them. The children and Mrs Brimming alike jumped with fright.

Mrs Brimming staggered up and pummelled Gary's back. "Leave him alone, Gary! Don't! Haven't you done enough!"

Amidst all the confusion, Jack seized his opportunity. He yanked the door open and rushed in.

"Jack! Jack!" screeched Kiki in delight. But her cry alerted Gary. He whirled round and saw Jack holding his beloved bird in his arms.

"Run! Run!" screamed Dinah, and they raced back through the door, Jack hot on their heels.

Gary was distraught. He looked fiercely

at his mother as if she were to blame and then raced after them.

But he stopped suddenly at the door and pressed one of several green buttons on the wall.

Inside the tunnel the children were dismayed to see the portcullis grinding down in front of them.

"Quick, quick!" Lucy-Ann cried and dived beneath the closing gate. But the others didn't make it. Lucy-Ann stopped. The others were trapped. A sudden look of horror on her face warned the others. They turned. The hooded figure of Gary was gliding silently up the tunnel towards them.

CHAPTER TWENTY-THREE

"GIVE HIM KIKI!" shrieked Dinah.

"What? NO!" shouted Jack, horrified.

"It's what he wants!" cried Dinah.

Gary grew ever nearer. They could see his eyes glittering, even in the gloomy light.

"Jack!" urged Philip. "Please!"

Poor Jack was torn. He couldn't bear the thought of sacrificing Kiki to this fiend. And yet—

"Jack, you must!" said Lucy-Ann urgently.

There seemed nothing else he could do. Jack slowly held Kiki out towards the figure.

"Sorry, Kiki," he apologised.

Gary took a step forward and reached out to take the bird. But at the last minute, Jack snatched her away. He thrust her through the bars of the portcullis and she flew up the tunnel to safety. Jack turned to stare defiantly at the hooded figure. Gary roared, his face twisted in despair and anger. Suddenly, he stopped, turned abruptly, and seemed to melt into the wall.

"Where did he go?" said Dinah, peering

into the darkness.

"I dunno," said Philip, equally puzzled. They were both certain they hadn't passed another door.

Jack had turned back to Lucy-Ann.

"Go and get help!" he said urgently.

"But what about you?" she cried.

"The best thing you can do for us is to get help. Go and get Bill! Hurry!"

Lucy-Ann looked at him uncertainly, then turned and raced up the tunnel.

"Right," said Philip. "We've got to get this portcullis open."

"BILL!" Alison woke screaming his name. She leapt out of bed and, pulling on her dressing gown, she rushed out on to the landing and into the children's rooms.

"What's wrong?" said Bill, bursting out of his room.

"Bill! Oh God! I had the most awful nightmare. The kids are in danger. I just know they are! I'm sure they've gone back to the castle!"

Bill was already dressed and behind the wheel of the car by the time Alison ran from the house and climbed in beside him. As he turned to back out of the drive, his coat swung open.

"You have got your gun!" exclaimed Alison.

Bill looked at her seriously for a moment.

"Yes." He pressed the accelerator and they screeched out into the road.

"Oh, Kiki! There you are!" beamed Lucy-Ann. The parrot had been waiting patiently just round the bend. She hurriedly bent down to scoop her up but was puzzled when Kiki flew off again.

"What is it? " Lucy-Ann asked, peering back over her shoulder. "Oh, NO!"

The hooded figure had dropped from the roof of the tunnel and was now drifting relentlessly towards her. He was chuckling insanely.

Lucy-Ann turned and bolted, stumbling over rubble and tearing heedlessly through countless spider webs. She burst into the main passage and sprinted in the direction of the fireplace. Behind her she could hear his rasping breath and the same mad cackling.

At last she reached the entrance. To her amazement the fireplace was open. She rushed out and desperately pressed the stud. The gate began to glide shut but to her absolute horror, Gary's hands emerged from the closing entrance. She looked wildly around the room, then dashed into the library, dived under the nearest dust sheet and curled up shivering on a musty couch. She heard Gary's soft tread in the great hall and lifted her head a little. Dust whirled into her nose.

"Ahhh . . . tishoo!" She gasped and pressed her hand to her mouth to stop a scream escaping.

But Gary had heard the sneeze. He crashed the door open and stepped into the room. Lucy-Ann couldn't help herself. She began to whimper as she saw his shadow fall across the sheet – the shadow of his hand descending.

Gary flung the sheet aside, still laughing insanely. Lucy-Ann cowered away from him, transfixed with fear. He leant over her, resting his hands on the chair and gazing at her with a puzzled expression.

"Margaret? Margaret? Is it you?" he asked uncertainly.

"Oh, please! Someone! Help me! Help me!" said Lucy-Ann weakly.

Gary pulled back his hood.

Lucy-Ann gasped as she looked up at his horribly disfigured face. "No . . . I'm . . . I'm Lucy-Ann," she managed to stammer.

"I'm so sorry, Margaret," said Gary, bending his head apologetically.

Realising he seemed to have no intention of hurting her, Lucy-Ann grew more courageous. "So you should be – chasing people, scaring them. You should be ashamed."

"I am ashamed," he wailed. "I wanted to help you."

"If you want to help me, just go away and stop chasing people," Lucy-Ann said firmly.

Gary seemed to brighten. "Do you want to play hide-and-seek again?" he asked eagerly.

Lucy-Ann shifted uneasily on the chair. Slowly she said, "Yes. Yes, all right. You count to a hundred and I'll go and hide." She rose warily from the chair and started to move towards the door. Suddenly, she felt his hand grip her arm. She swivelled round.

"It's so good to have found you again, Margaret," he said, and smiled broadly at her.

Lucy-Ann managed a faint smile, and

with a strained cheeriness said, "A hundred now, and no cheating." She closed the door behind her and ran out into the entrance hall.

"Children! Dinah! Philip!"

"Allie!" shrieked Lucy-Ann, "I'm in here." She rushed to the front door and tried to pull back the bolt. She could hear Alison calling their names from outside.

The lock was very stiff, and to try and attract Alison's attention Lucy-Ann began to bang on the door with her fists, and shout at the top of her lungs.

"Margaret!"

Lucy-Ann froze for a second but then grasped the lock and desperately struggled to open it. "Aunt Allie! Help! Help!"

Gary gave a terrible cry of anguish and pressed his hands against his head as if in agonising pain. He pulled up his hood, turned, and headed back towards the fireplace.

"Open the door! Lucy-Ann, open the door!" came Alison's panic-stricken cry from outside.

With an almighty effort, Lucy-Ann finally managed to pull back the lock and fling the doors wide.

She launched herself into Alison's arms, crying, "The others are trapped! Hurry! This way!"

CHAPTER TWENTY-FOUR

"Oh no, not again!" wailed Dinah. They had at last managed to raise the portcullis and were making their way back along the passage when they heard the sound of running feet coming towards them.

Jack had found Kiki waiting in the tunnel and now gripped her tightly.

"Come on," he said and turned back towards the decontamination unit.

Mrs Brimming and the three men were still in a state of shock and didn't notice the three children slip into the room. But Gary had seen them and Kiki as he ran back along the tunnel. Only seconds later he burst through the door and lunged at Jack.

Mrs Brimming spun round and cried, "Give him the bird, boy! Give him the bird!"

"No, I won't!" yelled Jack and he flung Kiki into the air.

Gary uttered a long low agonising groan as the pretty bird was once more lost to him. As sorrow turned to white-hot fury he hurled himself at Jack.

"DON'T MOVE! LEAVE HIM ALONE!"

Everyone spun round to see who had

given the order.

Bill had his gun trained on the hooded figure and repeated the command. The room fell absolutely silent.

Suddenly, Lucy-Ann stepped between Gary and the gun.

"Lucy-Ann!" cried Alison, and tried in vain to snatch her back.

"Gary," said Lucy-Ann gently, looking up into his face.

"Margaret!" he sighed wistfully.

"Let him go. Please. For Margaret. For me."

With an awful moan, Gary loosened his grip and Jack wriggled free.

"I'm so sorry. Forgive me . . ." Gary murmured. His expression changed. It became deadly serious as he spoke urgently. "Please, you must leave here. It isn't safe." He raised his arm in a farewell salute and smiled. Lucy-Ann backed away from him into Alison's arms.

"Don't follow me," he commanded and glided into the airlock chamber.

"No . . . NO!" cried Mrs Brimming, her face contorted with grief. She rushed to the video monitors, tears streaming down her cheeks.

They all watched as the dark-hooded figure moved purposefully across the cavern and entered the radiation chamber. He approached the foul pool and slowly raised his arms above his head. Then, slowly, deliberately, he stepped into the flaming pool. He raised his eyes to heaven in a moment of pure ecstasy. The terrible flames flickered about him. And he was gone.

CHAPTER TWENTY-FIVE

"Well, what did Sir George have to say?" said Alison as she joined the children at the breakfast table. Bill slipped the mobile phone into his pocket and sat down. They all looked at him expectantly.

"You lot seem to have recovered quickly!" he said, smiling round at them. "I can hardly believe it all happened only last night!"

Alison arched an eyebrow. "Mmm. A clean bill of health for one and all. No clicks on the Geiger counter."

"Now, let me see . . . The Bright gang's in custody," reported Bill. "And the decontamination people will finish at the castle in a couple of weeks, so Mrs Brimming can move back in."

"Poor woman. She wasn't evil, just misguided," said Alison thoughtfully.

"And guess what?" said Bill. They all stared at him. "Gary's been found alive!"

"What!" they all shrieked.

"Apparently he struck an air pocket in a cave under the pool. Some potholers found him and brought him to the surface. He's getting the treatment he needs at last . . ."

They all gaped at him.

"And now," Bill went on in a different tone, "I'd like to apologise for being so devious, especially with you, Allie. I promise it'll never happen again."

She smiled at him. "It's all right, Bill, I understand."

The children grinned at them.

"I don't know what you're so happy about," said Alison. "As far as I'm concerned, you're still in disgrace."

Philip and Dinah hung their heads.

"They almost look as if they mean it, don't they?" Bill said with a smile.

They giggled.

"Uncle's got measles!" whooped Jack suddenly, grinning from ear to ear and waving Uncle Eustace's latest letter in the air.

"That man is really unfortunate, isn't he?" smiled Alison.

"It might be three weeks until he's well enough to come back!"

Lucy-Ann's eyes lit up and she turned to Alison. "Will that be all right?" she asked anxiously.

"Of course! It's wonderful news. Not that

your uncle has measles— Oh, you know what I mean!"

But the children didn't hear her. They were too busy leaping around the room, whooping with excitement.

"All's well that ends well!" screeched Kiki, bobbing up and down on her perch.

The
Enid Blyton™
Adventure Series

All eight screenplay novelisations from the Channel 5 series are available from bookshops or, to order direct from the publishers, just make a list of the titles you want and send it with your name and address to:

Dept 6,
HarperCollins*Publishers* Ltd,
Westerhill Road,
Bishopbriggs,
Glasgow G64 2QT

Please enclose a cheque or postal order to the value of the cover price (currently £3.50) plus:

UK and BFPO: Add £1 for the first book, and 25p per copy for each additional book ordered.

Overseas and Eire: Add £2.95 service charge. Books will be sent by surface mail, but quotes for airmail dispatch will be given on request.

A 24-hour telephone ordering service is available to Visa and Access card holders on 0141-772 2281.